SWEET TEA & WEDDING RINGS

RACHEL HANNA

CHAPTER 1

Kate scooped a spoonful of Sweet Charlene's Honey out of the jar and dumped it into her cup of tea. She loved drinking out of these antique cups that Mia said belonged to their great grandmother. They were so delicate that she was afraid she'd drop one and break it, but she adored looking at them with their little blue flowers. Smaller than modern tea cups and coffee mugs, they barely held a few sips, but she didn't mind refilling her cup when needed.

Today's tea was a blend of autumn flavors with hints of orange and ginger. A longtime coffee drinker, she'd started enjoying more hot tea now that they owned a honey company. There was just something about tea with honey. It was soothing to her soul.

"Care for some tea with your honey?" Mia joked.

She was sitting at the breakfast bar drinking her own cup of tea, although she still preferred coffee.

"You're one to talk! This isn't nearly as potent as that sweet tea you drink with practically every meal. I'm surprised you aren't bouncing off the ceiling all the time!"

Mia laughed. "You get used to it when you're raised that way. Momma used to put sweet tea in my baby bottle. In fact, I have a picture of me walking around with it hanging out of my mouth, clutching that little rubber nipple with my front teeth."

Kate rolled her eyes. "Have you been checked for diabetes?"

"Oh, hush!"

"Coffee, I need coffee..." Evie said, stomping down the stairs, her fluffy bunny slippers not helping to soften her footsteps. Her hair, sticking up all over the place, showed what a fitful night of sleep she'd apparently had.

"Sorry, sweetie, but we only have tea this morning."

Evie glared at her mother, her eyes red. "Seriously? Who drinks this much tea?"

"I think it's better for you," Kate said.

Evie groaned. "I need coffee. Stat."

Mia stood up and took Evie's hand, leading her to the breakfast bar. "Sit down. I'll make you a cup."

"Thank you, Aunt Mia. At least *someone* around here loves me."

Kate chuckled. "Yes, you really live a rough life. Why are you so tired, anyway?"

"I can't seem to get my sleep schedule back on track. At Dad's house, the kids would stay up until all hours. Now, I need to get back on schedule before school starts next week."

"Good idea," Mia said as she poured water into the coffeemaker.

"Do we have guests?" Evie asked, laying her forehead on the counter. She always asked, mainly so she knew whether she had to be on her best behavior or could walk around the house looking like a troll.

"Nope. Our busy season is over until after Halloween, so we probably won't see many people these next few weeks while school starts back. Gives us time to work on the honey business and take a break from the summer rush," Kate said, carefully washing her teacup and then setting it on the drying rack.

"Good."

"Not good," Mia interjected. "We need guests to pay money so we can keep this place open."

"Don't worry, sis. The new business is doing pretty good, so it will take up most of the slack until we get more reservations."

"Still, I wish we could get our name out there more. This is a B&B, after all. With no guests, we're just a big, costly house."

3

"Coffee..." Evie groaned again as she lightly tapped her forehead on the counter.

"It's coming," Mia said with a laugh. "Hang in there."

Just as Kate was walking toward the living room to sit down, her cell phone buzzed in her pocket. "Hello?"

"Is this Kate Miller?"

The voice on the other end was female, and she sounded very official. "Yes, it is. Who is this?"

"Hi, Kate. My name is Carmen Spencer. I'm the editor of Grits And Glory Magazine."

Kate froze in place. Grits And Glory Magazine was the premier southern magazine, having been founded just two years previous. Everyone raved about the travel, decor and food related articles in the magazine, and it was a coup to be featured in it. But she had no idea why this woman was calling her.

"Oh wow. Nice to meet you," Kate stammered, feeling like an idiot.

"And you as well. Listen, we've heard about Sweet Charlene's Honey and sampled it recently."

"You did?"

"Yes. Turns out one of our interns was visiting family in your area this summer and picked up a jar at a festival. She brought some back to give to our taste testers and then to me. It's amazing!"

"Thank you so much."

"I mean, I've always thought that honey is honey,

you know? But there's something different about this honey. What's your secret?"

Kate laughed. "I guess we just have good bees." *What a dumb answer,* she thought to herself.

"My reason for calling is that we'd like to do a feature story in the magazine."

"Really?" Kate's excitement caught Mia's interest. She slid a cup of coffee over to Evie, who had already dozed off with her head on the counter.

"What?" Mia whispered. Kate waved her away.

"Yes. But it would require one of our writers to come stay at your B&B for a few days to interview you and take some photos. Would that be possible?"

Kate's cheeks hurt from grinning. "Absolutely!"

"Great. How about sometime late next week?"

"That would be fantastic. We'll have a room ready!"

"Okay, great. I'll send you an email with some details and confirmation. Sound good?"

"Sounds wonderful. And thank you so much for calling!" As Kate pressed end, she stood there stunned.

"What was that about?" Mia asked.

Kate smiled. "Our lives are about to change."

MIA STARED out over the mountains in front of her. They never ceased to amaze her. The best description she'd ever come up with was a blanket of blue carpet. That's what it looked like to her. Of course, those blues and greens would soon turn to yellow and orange as fall approached. She loved when that happened too. It meant more tourists, which was great for business, but it also gave her such a sense of peace.

Her mother had loved fall, with its crisp temperatures and beautiful views. They would often drive up and down the adjoining mountains, taking in each view like they'd never seen it before. She had photo albums full of pictures of her and her momma standing in front of those views. The tourists they met along the Blue Ridge Parkway were always more than willing to snap a photo for them. How she cherished those pictures now.

"What about this one?" Travis asked, holding his phone in front of her. She pulled her gaze away from the landscape in front of her and looked down at his phone.

"That one is beautiful. I love how you captured the orange color in the sunset and that purple tinge the mountains sometimes get in late day."

Travis smiled. "You're sounding like a real art critic."

"What can I say? I'm a woman of many talents," she said, laughing. He leaned over and kissed her cheek.

"Want me to name some other talents you have?"

Mia shook her head. "No. I want to eat this picnic basket full of food I made. I'm starving!"

They sat at one of their favorite spots over-looking a valley, a patchwork quilt underneath them. It was still warm enough to enjoy a picnic, even in the late afternoon. In a few weeks, that wouldn't be the case.

"What'd you bring?" he asked as she opened the enormous picnic basket she'd gotten as a Christmas present from Kate.

"Well, I made Momma's famous chicken salad with walnuts and pineapple."

"Yum."

"I put it in these pita pockets I bought. And I brought potato salad with that tangy mustard dressing."

"Sweet tea?" Travis asked, hope in his voice.

Mia stared at him. "Who do you think I am? Of course I brought sweet tea!"

They both laughed. "I've missed you lately. Sorry I've been so busy taking pictures."

"You never have to apologize for following your dreams, Travis. You know I support you."

"Another reason I love you."

"I *am* super lovable," she said, handing him a pita pocket filled with chicken salad.

"I do have some news."

"News?" She took a bite of potato salad and remembered her momma immediately. Charlene

7

could make anything, and potato salad was one of her specialities. Mia thought she was finally getting the hang of it.

"A gallery in Atlanta wants to buy some of my photos."

"That's fantastic!" Mia said, almost choking on her bite of food. She washed it down with a sip of tea. "Which ones?"

"There are a few, actually. We're having a video meeting in a few days to choose the ones they want to display."

Mia grinned. "This is a big deal, Travis! I'm so proud of you!" She leaned over and hugged him tightly.

The longer they were together, the more she could never imagine her life without him. When he'd come back into her life, she wasn't totally sure of where their relationship would go. Maybe some things in the past could never be undone. Turned out that their new relationship was better than anything she could've hoped for.

"Thanks. By the way, this chicken salad is amazing."

"If I can make it half as good as Momma, I'd be happy."

Travis chuckled. "You know, you don't have to turn into your momma to be an amazing woman in your own right."

"I guess so. She's just a hard act to follow." She

looked off into the distance again, remembering the time that she and her mom had sat in the very same spot one Easter. They'd had no guests at the B&B and decided to have a picnic. For hours, they'd eaten and talked and even played a few games of Scrabble. She sure missed her momma right now.

He reached over and squeezed her hand. "She'd be so proud of you, Mia. And Kate, too. I know she's looking down and smiling at both of you."

"I hope so."

EVIE LEANED BACK against the rough bark of the tree. She was glad to be back in her favorite spot overlooking the mountains. Cooper had built her the coolest tree platform, and she'd missed it over the summer while she was staying with her father in Atlanta.

"So, you're telling me they literally had no trees?" her friend, Dustin, asked.

"Not a one. Well, they had a little one they'd just planted, but God knows it will take twenty years to get tall enough to be called a tree."

"What'd you do there?"

"Went to the zoo. Watched movies. Played with my new siblings. Looked at stuff on my phone. Nothing major, really."

"Are you glad to be back?"

RACHEL HANNA

She nodded. "I am. I had fun with my new extended family, and I got to spend some good time with Dad, but this is my home now. I love it here."

Dustin laughed. "I guess it's pretty cool. But when you grow up here, all you want to do is leave as soon as possible."

"You want to leave?"

"Yeah. When I graduate, I'm going into the Army so I can travel the world."

"Aren't you scared of going to war or something?"

Dustin shrugged his shoulders. "Nah. Not really."

"I would be."

"What do you want to do when you graduate?"

"I don't know. I've got a couple of years to think about it."

"My mom says it will be here before we know it."

"Scary thought. I'm not ready to be an adult yet."

"Well, it comes whether or not you're ready. You need a plan."

"What if my plan is to stay here and help with the B&B?"

He shook his head. "There aren't enough people staying here to give you a job, Ev. You're going to need to go to college or something."

"I'm not really the college type," she said, sighing as she laid down against the cool planks of wood. It was getting near dinner time, and she expected to hear her mom calling for her at any moment.

"What type are you then?"

She giggled. "I have no idea."

"Better start thinking about it," he said, laying down beside her as they both stared up into the thick leaves at the top of the tree.

"Too much pressure. I'll think about it later."

* * *

COOPER WALKED to the other side of the lot. "So you want the driveway to come out over here, right?"

"Yeah." Mr. Pope was a man of few words. Older than dirt, he had finally bought the piece of property by the river that he'd wanted for most of his life. Now, he wanted to build a log cabin on it, and Cooper had been happy to snatch up the opportunity to build a house. Normally, he built decks and smaller buildings, but he was looking forward to spreading his wings a bit.

Thankfully, he'd been best friends with Mr. Pope's grandson in high school, so he'd gotten a referral. Even though Danny now lived in Austin, Texas, they'd connected on social media and one thing had led to another.

"And you want a wrap-around porch and deck overlooking the river?"

"I like to fish."

Man of few words for sure. Cooper had had a hard time getting much conversation out of the old man, but as long as his checks went through, he didn't mind too much.

"Me too. Trout fishing is good on this part of the river."

Finally, a slight smile. "You like to trout fish?" He eyed Cooper carefully, his big, bushy eyebrow raising higher, pushing his deep forehead wrinkles ever upward.

"Sure. I've caught many fish in that river."

"You didn't strike me as a fisherman. I thought maybe you were one of those feminine guys. What do they call them? Metro…"

"Metrosexual?"

"That's it. I saw it on a news show once. Them guys like to be all fashionable and smell nice. Some of them even get manicures! Anyway, I just don't understand a fella that don't like to fish. I don't mind smelling like a day at the river! I was never much of a hunter, but fishing is required for mountain men like us, I do believe."

Cooper struggled not to chuckle. "I think I can agree with that." Even though he didn't agree with a lot of old Mr. Pope's assessment of men who liked well manicured fingernails and not smelling like fish, he knew arguing would not change his mind. Plus, Cooper had never considered himself a "mountain man". He couldn't grow a beard to save his life, and plaid flannel shirts weren't currently occupying his closet.

"You think you can meet my deadline?"

"Yes, sir, I do."

"Good. I want to be in my new house as soon as possible. I probably don't have many years left, and I want them to be right here on this river."

"I understand."

"Do you?" Mr. Pope asked, looking at him carefully.

"Not sure what you mean?" Cooper said, feeling a bit uncomfortable.

Mr. Pope eased himself up onto the tailgate of his old red truck. It had been manufactured in the late seventies, and even though he'd obviously restored it at some point, the tailgate was already rusty again. "Do you know what it's like to be my age and just now chasing your dream?"

"I guess not." What else could he say?

"It feels… sad. It's exciting, but I feel like I wasted a lot of years doing what everyone else wanted me to do, you know?"

"Yes, sir."

Mr. Pope looked down toward the river. "I may not get a lot of time on that river, maybe a few years if I'm lucky, and I take those blasted pills the doctors keep pushing at me. High cholesterol, my fanny… Anyway, you young folks need to chase those dreams early."

"I'm trying…"

"No, you're not."

"Excuse me?"

He adjusted the way he was sitting and grunted a bit in the process. "Son, nobody dreams of building somebody else's house, especially not for this price."

"I think some people do dream of building houses," Cooper said, sitting down next to him.

"Maybe big neighborhoods, but not some old man's dream cabin. That's a job you take because you need the money."

Cooper had no idea why he was having such an in-depth conversation with a man he barely knew, but Mr. Pope reminded him of his late grandfather, and he'd been a man who gave great advice.

"Well, you sometimes have to start small..."

"Hogwash! Starting small just means waiting longer to achieve your dreams."

Cooper chuckled. "You're quite the motivational speaker, Mr. Pope."

"I just hate to see young folks make silly mistakes."

"So, what would you suggest I do?"

"Figure out what lights your fire and find a way to do it."

"Seems simple enough," Cooper retorted, trying not to sound sarcastic.

"It is simple. It just ain't easy."

Cooper thought about that for a moment. It wasn't easy. He sometimes felt a little lost in his life. He adored Kate and couldn't imagine life without her, but he didn't feel worthy. After all, he certainly didn't have a steady income to provide for a family. Mr. Pope might have been right. Maybe he wasn't taking enough chances. Maybe he was playing it too safe and would regret it.

CHAPTER 2

*K*ate pulled three more jars of honey from the shelf and set them on the worktable next to her desk. She rolled the first one in flexible cardboard and then in bubble wrap before placing it into the box. Then she started on the next one. This was something that had become old hat to her very quickly, and she could pretty much pack these boxes in her sleep now.

"I brought up some more boxes," Cooper said as he walked into the small office. Pretty soon, they'd have to expand. There was no way she could keep running the B&B and the honey business out of such a small space.

"Thank you," she said, barely looking up. She had three more orders to get ready before the mailman did his late afternoon pickup.

Cooper put the boxes down and walked up behind her, sliding his arms around her waist. "Stop."

"Stop what?"

He reached forward and stopped her hands from moving before slowly turning her around to face him. "Breathe."

"Cooper, I don't have time for this right now. Two of these orders are a day late."

"Breathe," he repeated. To appease him, she took in a quick breath, blew it out and tried to turn around.

"Not good enough."

"Fine," she grumbled. She closed her eyes for a moment, sucked in a deep breath and blew it out slowly. She would never admit that it felt good to take a moment and breathe.

"Now, listen to me. I'm here to help you, Kate. If you didn't hoard these orders and keep me from knowing about them, I would have helped you yesterday. Why do you keep trying to do everything yourself?"

She sighed. "I know you have things to do. This isn't your business. This was all my idea. I can't even saddle Mia with it."

"She's your sister, and it's her business too."

"I know. But, I got us into this, and I feel like it's mine to deal with."

"Kate, you need to let people help you."

"You can help me carry these down once they're

packed. How about that?" She turned around and went back to packing.

He chuckled. "I feel like I'm just muscle to you."

"Cute muscle, though."

Cooper walked over and sat on the edge of the desk. "So, why the more frenzied pace today?"

"I told you about the magazine piece, right?"

"Yes. And I am so proud of you."

"Well, the hope is that we will get slammed with orders after that, so I want to be caught up."

"When's the reporter coming?"

"Thursday. And then staying the whole weekend."

"Are you nervous?"

Kate looked at him. "Terrified."

He stood up and pulled her into an embrace, her cheek resting against his chest. "You're going to do great because you're a rockstar, Katie." She kind of loved when he called her Katie. It made her feel like a cute young cheerleader.

"I hope you're right because this is a pretty big deal for us, and not just for the honey business. The B&B will also be featured, and that could be fantastic for us."

He cradled her cheeks and looked down at her. "Let us help you with this, okay? If you get a bunch of orders, we all want to help. Even Evie and Travis can lend a hand. All right? Nobody is in this life alone, including you. Got it?"

She nodded. "Got it. Thank you for reminding me that I'm not alone."

"Sweetie, you'll never be alone as long as I draw breath."

She sank back into his arms and wondered what she had done to deserve a man like this one.

* * *

"DO YOU HAVE YOUR NOTEBOOKS?" Kate asked as Evie stood in the entryway, a look of irritation on her face.

"Yes, Mom…" she groaned. "I have everything."

"What about your lunch? Mia packed you a chicken salad sandwich and…"

"I have my lunch."

She stopped and looked at her girl. She remembered the first day of kindergarten and how big Evie's backpack looked slung over her little shoulders. Now, a junior in high school, Kate was all too aware that the days of sending her daughter off to her first day of school were drawing to a close. It made her tear up.

"You sure you don't want me to drive you?"

"I told you that Dustin is picking me up. No offense, but I don't want my mommy driving me to school."

Kate tried not to be offended, but she couldn't help feeling that way, at least a little bit. Her daughter was growing up and needing her less and less.

"Okay, well, give me a hug at least."

Evie rolled her eyes and then laughed as Kate wrapped her arms around her. "Bye, Mom."

"Have a good day!" Kate called as Evie shook her head and closed the front door. Kate walked to the window and peeked through the still closed blinds, watching as Evie got into Dustin's blue pickup truck and drove up the driveway.

"She'll be fine, you know," Mia said from the kitchen. She was making breakfast for the two of them, and Kate was secretly hoping she had the ingredients for mimosas because she needed a little something for her nerves this morning.

"I know, I know," she said, as she walked over and sat down at the table. "It's just hard knowing that next year she'll be a senior. And then she'll be all grown up and won't need me at all anymore."

Mia looked up from the pan of scrambled eggs she was making. "You know that's not true. I still needed Momma right up until the day she took her last breath. Evie will always need you. It'll just change."

"I don't enjoy change all that much," Kate said, chuckling.

"That makes two of us."

"The magazine reporter gets here around lunchtime," Kate said. She would never understand why the local school system had started on a Thursday of all things, but at least it would keep Evie occupied for a bit while the reporter settled in.

"Are you excited?" Mia asked as she slid a plate of scrambled eggs and bacon over to her sister.

"Excited? Hmm. More like petrified."

"Why? This is a great opportunity for us!"

Her sister's perky personality was a little too much this morning. Kate preferred well-controlled anxiety. "I know it's a great opportunity, but don't you feel the least bit freaked out that we're going to be featured in a national magazine? What if we say the wrong thing and look like two idiots?"

"It wouldn't be the first time I've looked like an idiot, sis. And besides, you're great at stuff like this. You thrive under pressure."

"That's not necessarily a great quality, Mia," she said.

"You want some advice straight from Momma's lips?"

Kate smiled. "Can you channel her spirit?"

"Kind of," Mia said with a laugh. "She drilled this stuff into me for over thirty years."

"Okay, what would Mom say?"

"She would say, 'Kate, you can handle this. The very fact that God put it in your path means you have exactly what it takes to make this great!'"

Kate felt that in her soul, as if her mother really

did just speak through her sister. "Thanks," she said, feeling tears welling up in her eyes.

Mia reached across the table and squeezed her hand. "I sure wish Momma could've met you. She would have been so proud."

Kate nodded and smiled. "I feel her here in this house and any time I'm with you. Next best thing, I suppose."

* * *

"REMEMBER that everyone needs a separate notebook for journaling, and you'll also need colored pencils. Check the portal online to see your journal topics for next week. Class dismissed!"

Evie liked all of her teachers this year, but especially Mr. Spectral. Not only did he have a cool last name, but he was easygoing and on the younger side. She thought she might enjoy Language Arts this year.

As she walked out into the hallway, her eyes searched for Dustin. Her only real friend, he provided some comfort to her. At first, she thought they might get together as girlfriend and boyfriend, but then they settled into the best friend zone and that idea was lost in the recesses of her mind. It was much better to have a best friend than a temporary boyfriend. If they broke up, she'd be all alone again.

She turned to head toward her locker, certain

Dustin would wait for her so they could walk to history class together. His class was directly across the hall from hers.

Just as she turned, someone ran straight into her, making her feel like she'd just been hit by a truck. She slammed against the pale yellow walls of the hallway as the wind was knocked out of her lungs.

"Oh my gosh, I'm so sorry! Are you okay?"

Evie looked up to see the most gorgeous guy she'd ever seen. He was taller than anyone she knew, and he had sandy blond hair and the kind of blue eyes that looked like pools of ocean water. She half expected to see a little fish swim by.

"Um... yeah... totally fine..." she said as she tried to stand up straight. Instead, she winced as her ankle gave way and she fell. The stranger dropped his backpack and caught her by her arms.

"You're hurt. Let me take you to the nurse's office."

Before Evie could respond, the guy somehow picked her up along with both of their backpacks and started toward Mrs. Dalrymple's office. She'd been the school nurse for over twenty years, and she looked like she should've retired ten years ago. Evie wasn't exactly confident about her nursing skills, at least beyond giving out headache reliever and ice packs for feverish students.

"It's fine, really. Probably just a sprain..."

They arrived at the nurse's office, and he carefully placed her down in a chair. He knelt beside her and smiled. "I really am sorry. Today is my first day here, and I was rushing to find my locker like an idiot."

She couldn't be mad at this guy. He was too beautiful. Maybe she was hallucinating from the pain and he was really Big Teddy, the weirdest guy in school who carried a plush T-Rex stuffed animal in his backpack for no apparent reason. They were about the same height...

"I'm Kieran."

Kieran. Dear God, that was an amazing name. Like some romance novel hunk.

"Evie."

"Nice to meet you, Evie," he said, his pearly white teeth shining in the bright fluorescent lights of the small nurse's office. For a moment, she swore she heard romantic music playing in the background as they looked at each other and then...

"What's going on here?" Mrs. Dalrymple asked, her hands on her very large hips. Today, she wore a long, pleated skirt that looked to be from the eighties - possibly the 1880s - with its loud colors and geometric shapes. Her button-up silk top with the large gold cat brooch really added to the ensemble.

"I stupidly ran into her in the hallway, and I think she sprained her ankle."

Mrs. Dalrymple looked at him for a moment. "I don't think I've seen you before."

"I'm Kieran Davis. I just moved here with my dad. We're from Tennessee and…"

"I don't need your full history, son," she said, holding up her stubby hand. Evie wanted to hear his full history. Heck, she would've gladly listened to him recite her whole US history book. His voice was thick with a southern accent, but a different one than she'd heard before. The people of Carter's Hollow definitely spoke with an accent, but she'd learned that different parts of the south had different accents. And his was full of twang and substance. Like thick molasses. His accent warmed her blood up so much that she could feel her face flushing. "What's the matter with you?"

"I think I sprained my ankle."

"Actually, I sprained her ankle. Totally my fault," Kieran interjected. She kind of liked this guy's gallant demeanor.

"Let me get some ice," Mrs. Dalrymple said, waddling into the adjoining room that had a little freezer.

"It's really no big deal," Evie insisted, although her ankle throbbed, and she was struggling not to cry.

"Evie? Are you okay?" Dustin suddenly said from behind her.

"I'm fine. Just sprained my ankle, I think," she said. Dustin walked closer.

"Who are you?"

Kieran reached out his hand. "Kieran. I just moved here."

Dustin stared at him and didn't shake his hand, instead turning back to Evie. "When you didn't show up to meet me, I got concerned. Eddie said he saw some big guy carry you the other direction."

"Some big guy?" Kieran said under his breath.

"Well, Kieran and I had an unfortunate first meeting in the hallway," Evie said with a giggle. Dustin was seriously cramping her style right now.

"I'll stay with you. You can go," he instructed Kieran.

"I caused this, so I don't mind staying."

Dustin glared at him. "No, it's cool, man. Wouldn't want you to get in trouble on your first day of school. I've got it from here."

Evie had never heard that tone in Dustin's voice before. It was more than a little odd, not to mention the fact that she wasn't ready for Kieran to disappear from her life. But her ankle was really throbbing, and she didn't have the energy for an argument.

"Here we go," Mrs. Dalrymple said as she walked up with an ice pack. She handed it to Evie and then stared at the two boys in front of her. "This isn't a group event, gentlemen. Why don't you both head to class now?"

"I can wait with her," Dustin said.

"So can I," Kieran retorted.

"Good Lord, you've got quite a fan club here. Regardless, both of you need to go to class. Now. She'll be here resting her ankle for a while."

Reluctantly, Kieran and Dustin walked toward the door. Evie leaned back in the chair, raised her leg onto the step stool Mrs. Dalrymple brought over and put the ice pack on her ankle.

"I'll meet you at our regular place after school, Ev," Dustin said as he started to leave.

Evie said nothing, leaned her head back and closed her eyes.

* * *

"I'll take my usual," Travis said, handing the menu back to Diane, his favorite server at the cafe. He'd been coming here and getting the same meal for years, but Diane still continued to hand him the laminated menu every single day. It was a running joke between them now.

"Sure thing, hon," she said, turning to a forlorn-looking Cooper. "What'll you have?"

"Roast beef sandwich on white, double fries and a large sweet tea. Oh, and one of those double chocolate chunk cookies." She eyed him for a moment and took his menu.

"Jeez, man, are you trying to plump up?" Travis asked with a chuckle.

"Stress, I suppose."

"What's got you so stressed that you're carb loading?"

"I guess I've just been thinking a lot lately."

"About?"

"The future."

"What about it?"

"Where am I going? What am I really doing with my life?"

"Didn't you get that building job with Mr. Pope?"

"Yeah, but that's one job. And the fact is, I can't support a family just doing odd jobs here and there. I mean, Carter's Hollow isn't exactly a happening place for contracting work. Most of these people have lived here forever, and they don't like a lot of change."

"Wait. Go back to that whole 'supporting a family' comment. Are you thinking of proposing to Kate?"

Cooper smiled slightly. "I've been thinking about that since the day we met."

"That's awesome, man!"

"No. It's not awesome. I need something to offer her and Evie. She's killing herself working so hard at the B&B and the honey business. And all I'm doing is the occasional gazebo or deck."

"You're building Mr. Pope's house!"

Diane walked to the table and set two large glasses of sweet tea down before walking away. "I know, but that's one job. And when it's over, I'm right back to where I started."

"I get what you mean, honestly. I mean, a gallery in Atlanta wants some of my pictures, but who knows if anyone will buy them?"

"That's great, man! And you have the book you did too."

Travis laughed. "Book royalties on a photography book… yeah, not a huge moneymaker, as it turns out. I mean, it's nice to have my name on a book, but I won't be retiring from it."

"It's still cool."

"You know, I think about popping the question to Mia all the time."

"Why don't you?"

Travis smiled. "Pretty much the same reason. I don't have a lot to offer. And I know we want kids. How could I support a kid just doing my photography?"

"Mia just wants you to follow your passion."

"I'd never give up photography, but I need a more regular income."

Cooper took a sip of his tea and sucked in a breath before slowing blowing it out. "I may have an idea."

"What kind of idea?"

Diane walked over with both of their plates and set them on the table. "Anything else, boys?"

"No, but thanks," Cooper said, waiting for her to walk away.

"Well? What idea?"

Cooper smiled. "A *big* idea."

CHAPTER 3

K ate stood at the front window, her nose almost pressed against the glass. She could see her breath fogging up the windows.

"You realize the alarm will go off when he pulls in the driveway, right?" Mia asked as she read a magazine on the couch. Cooper had installed a state-of-the-art gadget that set off a bell in the house when someone pulled into their long driveway.

"I don't trust it," she said, craning her neck. "What if he shows up and we aren't prepared?"

"Kate, we're over-prepared. We've cleaned this place top-to-bottom, and we've made so much extra food that we could feed the Georgia National Guard!"

As if on cue, the bell chimed and Kate started panicking a bit. "Are you sure we're ready? I mean, this is a huge national magazine, Mia. If we say the wrong thing…"

Mia stood up and put her hands on Kate's shoulders. "We've got this, sis. Momma is looking out for us, and you can't have a better angel on your shoulder. Trust me."

Kate sucked in a deep breath and slowly blew it out through pursed lips. "Okay. You're right, of course. It's all going to be fine."

A few moments later, they heard a car door shut. Mia held onto Kate's arm so she wouldn't press her nose to the window again. She didn't know why she was so incredibly nervous about this whole thing. After all, her parties and other events back in Rhode Island had been featured in magazines before. She'd even been interviewed a few times, too. But this felt riskier for some reason.

The doorbell rang. Mia and Kate looked at each other, smiled, and then walked toward the door. Kate opened it to find her first surprise. It wasn't a male reporter. It was a woman, and she was dressed to the nines with at least three-inch heels, a stunning - and obviously expensive - pantsuit and makeup that looked like it'd been put on by a professional in Hollywood. Her long blond hair was what Kate had always dreamed of, and she was carrying a purse that was pricier than all of Kate's clothes put together.

"Hello. My name is Olivia Steele. I'm looking for Kate Miller." She smiled slightly, but her demeanor was all business.

"I'm Kate. And this is my sister and business partner, Mia Carter."

She reached out her perfectly manicured hand. "Nice to meet you both. Mind if I come in?"

"Of course. Would you like us to get your bags?"

She shook her head. "No, that's okay. We can take care of that later. I assume they're safe in the car. Doesn't seem like we're in much danger way out here." There was a definite tone in her voice, and Kate noted no hint of a southern accent.

They stepped back and allowed her inside, watching her reaction. She looked around the room and then turned to them, smiling slightly. She never fully smiled, just enough of one to let them know her face wasn't frozen. "Very cute."

"Thanks. That's what we were going for," Mia said. There was a hint of irritation in her voice, but hopefully Kate was the only one picking up on that.

"So, how many guests will you have this weekend?"

Kate cleared her throat. "Just you."

Olivia's eyes widened. "Just me? Are you often empty like that?"

"We have a lot of repeat visitors, but this time of the year is a bit slow as families are focused on

33

starting back to school," Kate explained. Olivia pulled out an iPad and wrote something with some kind of special pencil. "But, it will pick up soon, for sure."

"I see. And you run the honey business out of here?"

"We do. Right now, we're still small enough that…"

"Good. So, how long have you had the B&B?"

"My mother opened it when I was a kid," Mia said.

"But the honey business is new?"

"Right. Just a few months, actually," Kate said proudly.

"Can I ask you something without you getting offended, Miss Miller?" She closed her iPad case and held it against her chest.

"Sure."

"Did you have an inside contact at Grits And Glory?"

"No. Why?"

"Well, it's just very unusual for such a small and new company to garner the attention of a well-respected national magazine like this. It seems out of the ordinary, to be honest."

"Can I ask you a question, Miss Steele?" Mia interjected. Kate's stomach churned.

"Of course."

"Are you from the south?"

Olivia chuckled. "No. I grew up in Southern California, actually. That's the only 'south' I know."

"I see. That makes sense then."

She looked at Mia for a long moment. "What makes sense?"

"Your lack of accent. And your lack of manners."

"Mia!" Kate said through gritted teeth. "I'm so sorry. She didn't mean that. Of course geography has nothing to do with manners!"

Mia crossed her arms. She was little, but she was feisty when she wanted to be.

Olivia waved her hand. "It's fine. Offending me is almost impossible. I have a very thick skin. Look, I'm going to be honest with you. This is a fluff piece that my editor gave me at the last minute because Craig Galvin, the original reporter, had a family emergency. G&G is a stepping stone for me. I was between jobs, this position opened up and here I am. But it's not exactly hard news. I mean it's mostly fatty dessert recipes, off-the-beaten path destinations like this and the occasional hard-hitting piece like poverty in Appalachia or spotlighting some animal rescue."

"Then why did you agree to come here?" Mia asked, her arms still firmly crossed.

"Because it's my job, for now anyway. And I don't mean to be rude, but I'd like to get this story done and move on. No offense."

"Oh, sure. Why would we take offense?" Mia said, rolling her eyes. Kate squeezed her arm.

"And I'd like to be honest with you. This is important to us. It's a tremendous opportunity for our honey company and for the B&B," Kate said, still squeezing Mia's arm in an attempt to keep her quiet.

Olivia smiled. "I understand your concern, but please also understand that I consider myself a journalist, not just a magazine reporter. I don't do fluff pieces. This article will be very different because I'm writing it. Craig would've written a sweet piece about two sisters running a B&B and selling honey. That's not me. I'll be watching your operation closely, maybe asking some harder-hitting questions and delivering a piece of *journalism* to my editor. Think of me as a fly on the wall this weekend, watching everything you do with a keen eye." With that, she turned toward the front door and walked down the steps to retrieve her bags.

"More like a snake watching us," Mia muttered. Kate couldn't help but agree with her.

"So, how did you get rid of her?" Travis asked as Mia poured him a cup of coffee. She'd spent the last fifteen minutes explaining her hatred for this woman.

"Kate is showing her the office and letting her

taste test the honey. I think she's trying to keep me away from her. Probably a good idea."

Travis took a long sip of the coffee and set it on the counter, his forearms resting against the breakfast bar as he sat on the stool. "Do you need me to do anything?"

"Just be on your best behavior," she said, leaning over and kissing his cheek.

"Always."

They both jumped when they heard a bang on the door. Mia ran over and opened it to find Evie standing there with a pair of crutches. "Oh, my gosh! What happened?"

Her friend Dustin was standing beside her, helping her into the house. Evie looked exhausted. "I had a minor accident at school. Dustin loaned me his crutches." Mia and Dustin helped her onto the sofa. She leaned her head back and sighed. "My armpits are already killing me."

"How did this happen, kid?" Travis asked as Mia helped Evie elevate her ankle on a thick throw pillow.

"I'll tell you how. Some new kid who's fifty-feet tall ran into her. She hit a wall and somehow sprained her ankle."

"He didn't mean to, Dustin," she said, rolling her eyes.

"Whatever. He better stay away from you," he mumbled.

Mia eyed them carefully. For two people who were just friends, there seemed to be some jealousy in the air right now.

"Why didn't the school call your mother? She would have been right over."

Evie looked up at her aunt. "Because I knew that the reporter was coming today. Besides, it's just a little sprained ankle. It's not like I broke my leg or anything."

"How do you know it's only sprained?" Mia asked, kneeling down and lightly touching her ankle.

"The school nurse looked it over, and she said to just elevate it and put ice on it this evening. If it's still swollen tomorrow or it turns any weird colors, I'm supposed to go to the doctor." As with any teenager, Evie seemed unbothered by her predicament.

"I better go upstairs and get your mom," Mia said.

"Is the reporter here?" Evie asked in a whisper.

"Yes. And she's not very nice. She's upstairs with your mother in the office."

She waved her arms. "Don't interrupt them! There's nothing she can do for me right now except worry, and I don't want her screwing this up because she's so focused on me."

"I guess you're right. Let me get you a bag of peas out of the freezer. That's always the best thing to use instead of ice."

Travis sat down in the chair next to Evie. "So tell

me who this guy is that did this to you. Do I need to go rough him up?"

Evie rolled her eyes. "No. Dustin is being overly dramatic. He's just this new kid at school. He got lost in the hallway, turned around and bumped into me. Totally an accident."

"I don't like him," Dustin said, under his breath but loud enough for anyone within a one-mile radius to hear.

"Sounds like my friend Dustin here doesn't like the guy."

"Dustin doesn't like anybody, especially if they're trying to be friends with me," she said, cutting her eyes at him.

"Here you go," Mia said, leaning over and placing the peas on Evie's ankle. She winced.

"How long do I have to keep this on here?"

"Fifteen minutes. Then take it off for fifteen minutes and do it again. Momma always said that helps to take away the inflammation." It seemed like Mia always had little nuggets of wisdom that her mother had imparted to her over the years. It made her feel safe to repeat those things.

"Oh, my Lord! What on earth happened?" Kate said as she came running down the stairs. "You're hurt? How in the world did you get hurt?"

Olivia was standing at the bottom of the stairs, all business as usual, holding her tablet against her chest. Mia could tell she was trying to stay out of the way, but part of it was probably that she didn't have any humanity in her body.

"I'm fine, Mom. Just sprained my ankle. Everything is okay," Evie said, her teeth gritted as she spoke softly. It was apparent that she just wanted her mom to get back to business.

"If we hurry, we can get to the urgent care center before they close for the afternoon. I don't know why they don't stay open later. It's ridiculous…"

"Mom. Listen to me. I'm fine. I'm going to keep this ice on my ankle… Well, this bag of peas… Anyway, I'm going to keep it here and chill out. I promise you, nothing hurts and I'll be fine."

"How did this happen?"

"Can we talk about this later? I kind of want to take a nap." It was obvious to Mia that she was lying and just trying to get rid of her mother, but she was doing a pretty good job of it.

"Okay. If you're sure. I was just going to walk Olivia out to the beehives and show her our setup."

Mia looked at her sister and noticed how tired she appeared. It was obvious that this reporter was draining every bit of energy out of her.

"I'll see you later," Evie said. Kate leaned over and kissed her on the head quickly before walking out the front door, Olivia and her expensive high heels clomping along behind her.

"Wow," Evie said, looking up at Mia. "That woman looked like a first class witch."

Mia giggled. At least Evie always told it like it was.

* * *

"I'M ABSOLUTELY EXHAUSTED," Kate said, laying back on her bed, staring up at the whirling ceiling fan above her.

"I bet. You were going nonstop all day," Cooper said. Hearing his voice on the phone after a long day was one of her favorite things, although feeling his strong arms around her was always better. Tonight she just hadn't felt up to having company.

"Sorry if I've been too busy to spend time with you. As soon as this reporter leaves, I'll be all freed up."

"Sounds heavenly," he said. "When does she leave?"

"You know, I have no clue. We didn't put an end date on her reservation, but I think she wants to get out of here as quickly as possible. She's not impressed with our neck of the woods."

"Did I just hear a northerner say 'neck of the woods'? We're going to turn you into a southerner yet!"

Kate laughed. "Seems that way."

"Look, you sound beat. Why don't you go take a nice, hot bubble bath and then get some sleep? You can even light that new candle you got at the festival."

She yawned. "I hate to cut our conversation short…"

"Katie, it's not a big deal. Get some sleep. We'll talk tomorrow. In fact, I'll come by for breakfast, okay?"

She smiled. "Can't wait. Love you."

"Love you too."

She laid there a few more minutes, feeling a sense of gratitude for her life, but especially for Cooper. She was thankful for the B&B, her newly found sister and father, her daughter and so much more. Life had changed so quickly, but for the better.

She couldn't stop thinking about the idea of a hot bath, even though she could barely keep her eyes open. "Maybe just a short one," she said to herself as she stood up and walked to the closet to retrieve her plushest robe. Something about getting away from Olivia Steele was more than appealing and washing off this day in a bubble bath seemed like a good plan.

Just as Kate walked past the window, she heard a noise. It sounded like a large bug hit the glass with a forceful thump. She paused for a moment, but thought little of it as she headed toward the bathroom. Then another thump. That was way too coincidental unless this bug was suicidal or something.

A little scared, she picked up a vase, as if that was going to help her protect herself from an armed intruder throwing things at her window. Now she really wished she'd accepted Cooper's invitation to go to the shooting range. Guns had never been her thing, but she was wishing she had one right now.

Finally screwing up her courage, she crept over to the window and peeked through the side of the drape. She saw no one. Now, she was freaked out. Maybe it was a ghost, although she didn't believe in that kind of stuff. Just as she finally let out a breath, Mia burst into her room.

"Did something just hit your window?" she asked, breathless, her hand on her chest.

"Oh my gosh, yes! You too?"

Mia ran into the room, shutting the door behind her. "I was scared to death. Somebody got down here without the driveway alarm going off. Should we call the police?"

Kate thought for a moment. "That magazine reporter is here. The last thing we need is for her to write a big story about how our B&B isn't a safe destination. We'd be dead in the water."

Mia stared at her. "Very poor choice of words."

"Where's Evie?"

"In bed. So is Olivia, as far as I know."

"We need a gun. Or a big, burly man."

"Or a big, burly man with a gun," Mia suggested.

They froze in place for a moment longer before Kate couldn't take it anymore. "We have to be brave. Let's go downstairs and see if anything looks amiss."

"Maybe we should call the police, Kate."

She turned and looked at her. "Do you want our business to implode because we heard a bug hit the window?"

"It wasn't a bug."

"We don't know that. Come on."

They tiptoed down the staircase. The living room and kitchen were dark, only the light of the moon coming through the windows. "Don't turn on the lights. They'll see us plain as day," Mia said.

Kate pulled her phone from her pocket and used the flashlight, being careful to only aim it downward so it wouldn't be too obvious to anyone lurking around outside.

After peeking out the front windows, they saw nothing, so they headed to the kitchen windows in the back of the house. When Kate looked out the window over the sink, she saw something. Or someone. A figure standing right beside the deck Cooper had built for them. The person was wearing a dark-colored hoodie and dark pants.

"Oh, no. It's a burglar. We're going to have to call the police," Kate said. This was bad. And dangerous. They'd just have to do damage control for the business later.

"Hand me your phone," Mia said. Before Kate could give it to her, the person approached the sliding glass door next to the breakfast area and waved. Wait. They waved? What kind of burglar waved?

"Why is the homicidal maniac waving at us?" Kate whispered as they froze in place staring at the person.

"I don't know, but should we smile? I feel like we should smile and wave back. Is that because I'm southern?" Mia asked, speaking through her lips like she was a ventriloquist.

"Let me in!" the person said in a loud whisper. At least now they knew she was female. She was also petite in stature and looking less scary by the moment. Of course, she could have a gun in her pocket or a machete in her pants' leg. Kate decided maybe she'd watched one too many thriller movies with Cooper.

"Who are you?" Mia called back.

Finally, the woman pulled down her hoodie and took off the dark glasses she was wearing.

"Lana?" Kate said, her mouth hanging open. Lana Blaze, one of the world's most famous singers and multiple Grammy winner, was standing at their back door. Since having her wedding there months ago, they hadn't seen or heard from her, and honestly they never expected to.

"Yes. Can you open the door? There could be bears out here!"

Mia rushed over and unlocked the door before

sliding it open. She looked just as shellshocked as Kate did.

Lana stepped into the house and unzipped her jacket before removing it and hanging it over the back of one of the chairs. She ran her fingers through her hair, trying to fix it. It was funny to see her without all the makeup and superficial stuff. Normally, Lana was one of the most fashionable celebrities in Hollywood with her designer clothing and wild outfits. Right now, she had on a pair of simple black jeans, black ankle boots and a light gray t-shirt.

"Well, hey, girls!" she said, a big smile on her face. She hugged Mia first and then Kate before stepping back.

"Lana, what on earth are you doing here? At night? Dressed like a burglar?" Kate asked, more than a little confused.

Lana chuckled. "I'll be glad to explain my antics to you ladies, but can I have a glass of wine first? You got anything good?"

Mia stared at Kate for a moment. "Um, sure. White okay?"

"Anything is good right now. It's been quite a few days." She made herself at home in the living room, settling into an armchair and leaning her head back. Kate could see her let out a long breath and rub the bridge of her nose.

"What in the world?" Mia whispered to Kate as they stood close and out of view of the living room.

"I have no idea. Do you think she's on drugs or something?"

"I don't know, but this whole thing is weird. And the last thing we need is for Olivia to find her here. God forbid she is on drugs. Or what if she changes the whole story to being about Lana and away from our business?"

"How's that wine coming?" Lana called.

"On its way," Kate said, forcing a smile.

CHAPTER 4

*M*ia couldn't believe that she was sitting in her living room with Lana Blaze, at midnight, drinking wine like it was no big deal.

There had been no way that she was going to turn the woman away, not after her momma had told her to always welcome strangers into their home. Charlene had been the most welcoming person in the world, often offering meals and beds to people in need.

Of course, Lana Blaze was certainly not in need. She had more money than Mia would ever see in her lifetime. But right now, there was something about her that made Mia feel sad. She could tell Lana was struggling with something, although she was putting on a happy face. Mia figured that most celebrities had to do that, put on a smile even on the days they felt like crying.

"Lana, not that we aren't delighted to see you, but it is a little odd that you would unexpectedly show up at our door in the middle of the night dressed... like that... after throwing what I can only assume was rocks at our windows. Do you care to explain yourself?" Kate finally asked, obviously tired of tiptoeing around the subject.

Lana set her glass of wine on the table and smiled, albeit sadly. "Yeah, I guess I may have scared you ladies. But those weren't rocks. I wouldn't throw rocks at your windows! I found some walnut shells as I walked down the driveway."

"Why don't we start there? How did you get past the alarms at the end of the driveway?" Mia asked.

"Oh, that was easy. I'm pretty small, so I just stepped over the sensors."

Mia and Kate looked at each other and then laughed. "I guess we need to upgrade our security," Kate said.

"I know this might seem really crazy, but this was the first place I thought of coming after everything that happened."

"What do you mean? What happened?" Mia asked.

She looked at them quizzically. "You ladies must not read the tabloids."

Kate shook her head. "I know I don't. It all seems like a bunch of trash to me."

Lana laughed. "It is trash. But sometimes they hit the nail on the head, and in my case they did just that. My husband and I have separated."

"Oh, I'm so sorry," Mia said, reaching over and patting her knee. When she realized what she was doing, she drew back her hand. This was a celebrity, after all.

"I'm sorry too. That must've been devastating. I've been through a divorce, so I understand."

"Yeah, well, I was just shellshocked when it happened. Turns out he had been cheating on me with my manager. The same manager I've had for ten years, since I was a teenager and just starting out in this business. The same manager that encouraged us to get married and have the big, fancy wedding here."

"Yikes. She sounds like an awful person," Mia said, tilting her head to the side.

"Oh, it was all for show, anyway."

"What do you mean?" Kate asked.

"He wasn't my soulmate. He was just a good match to improve my branding. We knew going in that this would never work, but we both felt pressured. And I kept up my end of the bargain, not seeing anybody else, being the devoted wife. We were even thinking about having kids soon. I'm glad we didn't go down that road."

"I'm sorry about all of this, but I guess I don't understand how you ended up all the way across the country in the dark Georgia woods?" Kate said. Lana stood up and walked over to the mantle, picking up a picture of Mia and her mother.

"I noticed this picture when we were here for the wedding. When my stylist was brushing my hair right before I walked outside, I looked at it. I didn't have a good relationship with my mother. She was absent for most of my life but came back into the picture when I got famous. Or at least she tried to. My manager wanted me to make nice with her to give me a more squeaky clean image. I tried... for a while."

"You don't have a relationship with her now?" Mia asked.

"No. She brings a lot of negativity into my life, and I just don't want that. Anyway, when I looked at this picture, it made me sad. I was sad because I was marrying a man that I really didn't love. I was sad because I didn't have my family here because of the paparazzi always following them around. And I was just sad that I couldn't have a normal life, or at least some normal moments."

"Lana, what are you getting at here?" Kate asked. Mia got the distinct impression that Kate wanted to go to bed.

"I came here because it was the first place I thought of where I felt I could have some of those normal moments. Some quiet time to think about what I want to do next. I'm not sure I'm cut out for this business anymore."

"But you're Lana Blaze!" Mia said without thinking.

Lana smiled slightly. "See? You think of me as this special thing, this big star. I don't think of myself that way. I just wanted to be a singer. I wanted to stand on the stage and sing my songs. I had no idea it was going to require me to take on this alter ego."

"Alter ego? I thought you were being yourself." Kate said.

Lana shook head. "No. The general public is naïve about that. Everything you see me wear or do is completely coordinated by my handlers."

"Handlers? That makes you sound like some kind of circus animal," Mia said.

"And that's exactly what it feels like. I never have the opportunity to be myself. I'm never going to meet a man, settle down, have a family. Any man I meet is going to be completely focused on who I am in the public spotlight, my money, my fame. I don't get a break from it. Everywhere I go all over the world, people know who I am. Or at least they think they know who I am."

"How did you get here?" Kate asked.

"I rented a car under an assumed name and I drove. I parked a few miles down the road and then walked the rest of the way. It was a little scary in the dark, but I haven't felt this free in so many years. I feel like I can finally breathe. Walking through those woods alone in the fresh air, I felt a weight lift off of me. Nature doesn't care who I am."

Kate looked at Mia and then at Lana. "I'm not sure you're going to like what I have to say next."

Lana walked over and sat down, taking another sip of her wine.

"What do you mean?"

"We only have one guest here right now, and she happens to be a reporter for a national magazine on assignment to cover our business."

Lana's eyes widened. "You mean there's a reporter upstairs right now?"

"Yes. And if she finds out that you're here, we will never be able to protect you."

She sighed. "I'm not safe anywhere."

"We will do whatever we can to keep her from finding out that you're here, but right now we need to get you in a room. And you can't come out unless we tell you that it's safe, okay?" Mia said.

"I'm too tired to argue tonight. I just want a nice, soft bed away from the craziness that is my life."

"And that we can do," Mia said, smiling. She just hoped that she could keep her promise to Lana and make sure that Olivia Steele never found out that the world's biggest singing star was right down the hall.

* * *

EARLY MORNING WAS Cooper's favorite time of day. There was just something about the crispness of the mountain air mixed with the heat of the coffee in his insulated cup. He could feel fall coming around the corner, and there was nothing quite as beautiful as autumn in the Blue Ridge Mountains.

The leaves would soon turn all shades of orange and gold, showcasing a blanket of colors across the landscape. He loved how the sunlight danced off the mountains any time of year, but fall was his favorite. The smells were a part of that, of course, with smoke billowing from chimneys that dotted the ridge near the B&B. The smell of leaves burning was one of his favorites, too.

For now, the summer heat was still in full force, although it wasn't nearly as bad higher in the mountains as it was in the suburbs, and he sure didn't want to move to the suburbs or the big city. Mountain life was in his blood, and as long as Kate never left, he was happy.

"Sorry, I'm late," Travis said. "I got stuck on a call with the gallery in Atlanta. I've got to get Steve over at the office supply place to help me package up three framed prints for a show next weekend."

"Are you going to the show?" Cooper asked before taking another sip of his piping hot coffee.

"No, thank goodness. That's not my scene at all, but I would like to sell more prints."

"It used to be your scene, didn't it?" Cooper asked, propping his foot up on a tree stump.

"I guess so, but the longer I'm back home, the less I ever want to go into the city again."

Cooper laughed. "I was just standing here thinking the same thing, man. How could anyone choose the city, with all the traffic and noise, over this?" He waved his hand outward across the horizon, the morning pinkish-orange sky turning blue.

"I guess everybody likes different things, but I don't understand it either. Better for us, though, right? Who wants a bunch of city folks up here?" Travis said with a chuckle.

"Well, that's kind of why I brought you here."

Cooper had invited Travis to meet him at a piece of property just down the road from the B&B. It was mostly wooded with some river frontage and a beautiful view from one of the ridges, which is where they were standing now.

"Yeah, you've been kind of mysterious. What is this place?"

"You remember Sally Holcomb from high school?"

Travis thought for a moment. "That girl with the buck teeth and frizzy red hair?"

"Nah, that was Sally Hanson. Boy, she was something else, wasn't she?"

"Scary is what she was. I remember she was

really into Halloween and brought that shrunken goat's head to school."

"I heard she does tarot card readings now."

"That seems about right."

"Sally Holcomb's dad ran the trout fishing expeditions."

"Oh, that's right! I think his name was Stu?"

"It was. He passed away right after we got out of high school. Then Sally married some guy and moved to Savannah."

"What does that have to do with you bringing me here?"

"This was their land. Can you see those three little log cabins down there by the river?" Cooper pointed down the hill.

"Oh wow. I had no idea those were down there."

"They need some serious fixing up to be habitable again."

"And Sally hired you to fix them up?"

"No. Sally wants to sell this land. It's almost seventy acres."

"She wants you to find a buyer then?"

Cooper looked at him. "I want *us* to be the buyers."

"What?"

"You and me, business partners."

"You have to be out of your mind, Coop. First off, not that long ago we wanted to strangle each other.

And second, what would we do with such a large plot of land?"

"I think we've mended fences, unless you're still holding a grudge?"

Travis laughed. "Nah, but who knows what the future holds?" Cooper punched him in the arm. "But, seriously, what would we do with all this land and those cabins?"

"An adventure retreat!"

"A what?"

"People will pay good money to come up here and get a real mountain experience, Travis. With your knowledge of these mountains and my building experience, think of what we can do with this place! People will pay to come stay here, and we will take them on guided hikes and fishing experiences. We can even build a zip line, ropes course... And what about corporate business? There are so many options." Cooper could hardly contain his excitement and hadn't slept since Mr. Pope had told him about Sally Holcomb wanting to sell the family land.

"Look, man, I can see you're pumped up about this, but..."

"Travis, we both want to create more for our future families, right? I mean, if all goes well, we'll be brothers-in-law before it's all said and done. What better thing than a family business?"

"Mia and Kate already have a couple of family businesses."

"True, but this could change our lives, their lives, and even our future grandkids' lives. I just know this is a winning idea."

Travis leaned against a nearby tree and looked down at the cabins. "I'm a photographer, Cooper. That's what I do."

"You know as well as I do you can't make enough doing that. You've said so yourself. You're limited by wanting to stay here in Carter's Hollow. Look, you can still take pictures and sell them to galleries or whatever. But, this would also give you the chance to show visitors these mountains through your eyes."

"Okay, let's just say I even remotely entertain this idea. What do you think Kate and Mia are going to say?"

Cooper sighed. "Well, that's the part that you're probably not going to agree with."

"What is that supposed to mean?"

"I don't think we should tell them yet. In fact, I don't think we should say a word until we've bought this place and started working on the business plan."

Travis stood there, his eyes wide. "Are you insane?"

Cooper laughed. "Probably, but hear me out. We have some strong-willed women in our lives. And they also can see every potential problem in any situation."

Travis chuckled under his breath. "I don't think I would tell them that's what you think."

"Don't get me wrong. It's great that they are so smart and able to see around every corner, but I know Kate is very careful. She doesn't like to take a lot of risks. And she would definitely see this place as a tremendous risk."

"But if we're planning on building our lives with them, don't you think we should tell them about something this huge before we do it?"

"When I was a kid, I watched my grandpa. He was this larger-than-life character, and he loved my grandmother more than anything in the world. He owned a construction company, which is probably where I get my skills. Anyway, he wanted to buy this gigantic piece of equipment to help move earth easier. He didn't tell grandma, went out and bought it and then had to break the news to her."

"And how did that go?"

"At first, she was ticked off. She yelled so loud that we thought the house was going to cave in. But then my grandpa did something smart."

"And what was that?"

"Well, you see, before he told her about that big, expensive piece of equipment, he made sure to get extra business. Once he told some potential customers that he had a piece of equipment, they immediately hired him to do jobs. So he did them, came home and handed grandma a stack of money."

"And what did she say?"

"Not a lot after that. I think Kate and Mia will be

so proud of us if we buy this place, start working on it, and get some business coming in. After all, it can only improve their lives if we make this place a success."

Cooper could tell that Travis was giving it some serious thought, but he still looked hesitant. Travis had had a checkered past with Mia, and Cooper knew he didn't want to do anything that might mess up their relationship. Of course, he felt the same way about Kate. The last thing he wanted to do was jeopardize the bond they had, but he also had a strong need to take care of her and Evie for the long run.

"I'll tell you what. I'll give it some thought."

"I have a meeting with Sally tomorrow at three o'clock. We're going to be right here and walk some of the land, look at the cabins and so forth. If you think you're interested, be here at three. If not, I'll assume I have to do this alone, which will totally stink, but I'll understand."

Travis nodded his head. "I promise I really will think about it. I have to admit, it's an interesting idea."

Cooper softly punched him in the arm. "We could have a lot of fun, man."

Travis looked around. "Something tells me we're going to have a lot more work than fun."

CHAPTER 5

Olivia stared down at her plate with a look on her face like she had more questions than answers. "And what did you say this is again?"

"Cheese grits with bacon. I also put some bacon in the blueberry pancakes. How many do you want?" Mia asked.

"I guess... one?"

Mia stared at her. "You only want one pancake? I don't think I've ever met anyone in my life who only ate one pancake."

She put one on a plate, grabbed the fancy little syrup dispenser and slid them across the table. Part of her wanted to slide it hard enough for it to slam into Olivia's ample chest and stick to her for the rest of the day.

"Is this how you eat every day?" Olivia asked, still

poking at the grits like they were some sort of gruel she was being forced to eat.

"Not every day. Sometimes we have blueberry muffins or waffles or breakfast sandwiches..."

"Wow. Have you ever thought of a smoothie or maybe just an egg white omelette? I mean, most of the time I don't even eat breakfast. It's really an unnecessary meal, and this is a lot of calories."

"Momma said that breakfast is the most important meal of the day."

"Was Momma several hundred pounds?"

Mia stared at her again. It was taking all of her restraint not to run from one end of the kitchen to the other, slide across the table on her belly and strangle the woman.

"No. Momma was a petite, beautiful woman with more grace and elegance than most people will ever know. And she was a dang good cook. I'd like to think I can live up to that. In fact, people come from all around to stay here at the B&B and eat this food."

"I'm not trying to offend you, Mia. It's just that I'm not used to this type of food. Where I live, we eat very healthy. Very organic. There are vegan restaurants on every corner, and the gluten-free options are endless," she said, still picking at her food.

"You don't think this food is healthy?"

"You do?"

Mia leaned against the breakfast bar and crossed her arms. "I don't think it's just about the food. I think it's about the company. The laughter. The comfort. All of those are healthy things. Spending your life counting calories sounds like the definition of hell to me."

"Yeah, well, I guess we can agree to disagree," she said, finally taking a bite of the grits. She didn't cringe or start retching, so Mia considered that to be a good sign. "Can I get you something to drink? Coffee?"

"Too much caffeine."

"Orange juice?"

"Way too acidic. You should try to keep an alkaline state in your body for optimal health."

Mia rolled her eyes "Water?"

"I guess if that's all you have. But I prefer bottled."

"We only have tap water here. How about some sweet tea?"

"I've never tried sweet tea. It sounds intriguing."

Mia walked over to the refrigerator, pulled out the big pitcher and poured some into a small glass. She certainly didn't want to waste it on somebody who was likely to spit it across the room.

"Here you go. Now, if you don't mind, I have things to do."

"Actually, I wanted to see if maybe I could interview you today."

"Interview me? For what?"

Olivia took a small sip of the tea and then scrunched her nose. "Goodness! This tastes like sugar water. How about just get me a regular glass of water or maybe some almond milk?"

"We don't have almond milk. We get our milk from cows around here. I'll get you some water."

This woman was high maintenance. She was sure if she still had a dictionary in her house, Olivia Steele's picture would be right next to that term.

"Now, what's this interview you want to do?" Mia asked, as she handed her a glass of water. Olivia quickly took a sip, swirled it around in her mouth and swallowed like she was trying to get rid of poison.

"Well, Kate tells me you named the honey company after your mother. And since you are the only one who knew her, I thought it might be nice to sit down and have a chat about the namesake of your company."

Mia couldn't help but want to talk about her mom. Even though she wasn't on earth anymore, she still wanted everybody to know who Charlene was. Plus, that would give Kate time to bring Lana out of her room for a little while and get her a good meal. "Okay, fine. How about we sit out by the dock in fifteen minutes?"

"Sounds good. I'll finish my food, go freshen up and meet you out there."

As Mia walked up the stairs, mostly to pass a message to her sister, she wondered how this interview would go. Olivia didn't seem like she was a straight shooter. She always had an ulterior motive. And Mia was sensitive about her mom, So this could go either terribly well or just plain terrible. She figured if it went south, she was strong enough to push her straight into the lake.

KATE PRESSED her face into Cooper's chest, taking in the smell of his cologne. It seemed like years since she had been this close to him. Lately, it had only been a series of phone calls keeping them in touch. He was always busy with his building projects, and she was busy with the irritating reporter staying at her house.

"I can't believe you're finally standing here. Do you want some breakfast?"

He shook his head. "I actually got up early this morning and ate just so you didn't have to cook me anything."

"It's no bother. Mia actually cooked some food for Olivia this morning. I heard she wasn't too impressed with our way of cooking in the south."

Cooper chuckled. "No surprise there. She doesn't sound like the nicest person."

"Yeah, well, she's not. I can't wait until she leaves here."

"When will that be?"

"I have no idea. For somebody who seems to hate it here, I don't understand why she's not leaving."

"Where is she now?"

"Mia said they were meeting down on the dock to do an interview about our mom."

"Oh, she better be careful there. If she says one wrong thing, Mia is bound to push her into that lake."

Kate shrugged her shoulders. "Hey, if that's what's meant to happen, we have to let it happen." They both laughed. "Listen, I know you can keep a secret, so I have to tell you something."

He looked a little concerned. She took his hand and led him over to the sofa, sitting as close to him as she could while still making eye contact. "

"Okay, you're scaring me a bit."

"I have somebody upstairs in one of the rooms that I'm keeping hidden."

"You haven't started drinking that bottle of wine this morning, have you?"

She playfully slapped his arm. "I'm being serious. Lana Blaze showed up here last night out of the blue."

"Lana Blaze? The singer?"

"The very same one. Apparently, her marriage was a farce, and she is tired of being scrutinized all the time, so she drove cross-country and snuck onto the property."

"Wow. That's crazy."

"Besides Mia, you're the only other person who knows. We have to keep this quiet."

"I understand. Is there anything I can do to help you?"

She leaned in and laid her head on his shoulder. "The only thing you can do is just let me sit here with my head on your shoulder for a while."

"As long as you want to," he said, leaning his head onto hers.

* * *

EVIE OPENED HER EYES, surprised to see bright sunshine piercing through the window blinds. She checked her clock and realized that school had started a couple of hours ago. Her mom must have allowed her to stay home an extra day because of her ankle sprain, opting not to wake her up and allowing her to get some rest.

Now that she was awake, she felt the throbbing in her ankle. She pulled the cover back to make sure it didn't look red or swollen like the school nurse had instructed. So far, it looked just like her other ankle, but that didn't mean it didn't hurt.

She sat up on the edge of her bed, gently hanging her legs over the side. She was a little hesitant to put weight on her ankle for fear that it might be worse than she thought. The last thing she wanted was to have to wear a cast or get some kind of surgery. As she stood up, bracing herself against the bedpost, she felt like maybe it really was just a sprain. She could put most of her weight on it, although it was still pretty tender. She figured she would at least use the crutches for one more day. No need to rush herself and end up causing more harm to her ankle.

Hungry, she decided to head downstairs and see what she could find. She was pretty sure that her aunt Mia and her mom were probably out in town somewhere at this point. They usually ran errands during the day when they didn't have many guests staying at the B&B. Plus, they were probably trying to get away from that horrible reporter lady who was currently staying with them.

She grabbed the crutches that were leaning against the wall and headed out into the hallway. As she made her way down past the other guest rooms, she noticed the reporter wasn't there. Her door was standing open. She was probably walking around the property trying to pick out all of the ways that she hated it. Evie wished she would just go ahead and leave, and she worried that her mother was going to be way too attached to the outcome of the article being written.

Just as she passed the bathroom, the door opened, startling her. She almost dropped her crutches when she turned around and saw Lana Blaze standing in the hallway right in front of her.

"Oh! I didn't know anyone was here," Lana said,

pulling her towel tight around her. Although her hair was wet and she wasn't wearing any make-up, it was impossible for Evie not to know who she was. After all, she was one of Evie's favorite singers of all time.

"Lana Blaze? What are you doing here?"

Lana looked around like she was trying to hide from someone. "Your mom didn't tell you?"

"Tell me what?"

"Come in my room," Lana said, pulling on Evie's arm. They went into Lana's room and shut the door.

"Is everything okay?"

Lana smiled sadly. "Not really, kid. Enjoy your childhood because adulthood can suck sometimes."

"Why are you here? Is your husband here too?"

She shook her head. "No. It's a long, complicated story, but the basic premise is that I'm here hiding from my real life. I just need some time away, and your mother and aunt were kind enough to let me stay here."

"They didn't tell me you were coming."

"They didn't know. I sort of showed up without notice last night. Scared them half to death because I was throwing walnuts at the windows."

Evie stared at her for a moment. Throwing walnuts at the windows? That was not something she ever expected to hear Lana Blaze say.

"Well, I'm sorry if things aren't great right now, but it's really cool to have you here again."

She smiled. "Thanks. But I have to ask you to please not tell anyone. Nobody knows but your mother and your aunt Mia. If this gets out, especially to that reporter, my cover will be completely blown."

Evie nodded. "Don't worry. I won't tell a soul. And if you need some company while you're here, you know where my room is."

Lana laughed. "Thanks. I would like to get something to eat, but I'm not really sure where everybody is."

"Don't worry. I think the reporter is gone right now, but I'll go downstairs and check. I was going to make myself a late breakfast, maybe some eggs and bacon. Would you like some?"

Lana looked her up and down. "It doesn't look like you're in the best shape to be doing that. What happened?"

"Sprained my ankle at school yesterday. But I'm fine. I don't mind making us some food."

"Thanks."

Evie turned and started walking toward the stairs. "Hey, do you mind if we eat together? In my room or yours?"

"Sure. That sounds great."

She smiled as she turned around and started walking down the stairs. What a great turn of events to get to pick Lana Blaze's brain over lunch. She had lots of questions about what it was really like to live in Hollywood.

* * *

MIA SAT in the Adirondack chair overlooking the lake and the mountains. It was such a peaceful place, one of her favorite areas of the entire property.

Olivia had met her on the dock, as promised, but she was currently standing up taking pictures that would be used in the magazine article. It surprised Mia that she was using her phone, although the latest gadgets probably took better photos than expensive cameras, anyway. She finally walked over and sat down, crossing her legs in that pretentious way of hers.

"It's actually very nice out here," Olivia said, looking around at the blue tinged mountains that blessed the landscape of Carter's Hollow.

"You seem surprised about that. Do you think all beautiful things have to be in California or something?"

Olivia chuckled under her breath. "Of course not. California is a beautiful state with mountains and sunshine and snow and ocean. But there are lots of pretty places all over the world."

"I wouldn't know. I really haven't traveled much."

"Why is that?"

Mia shrugged her shoulders. "I don't know. I guess because I was helping my mom take care of this place, and then she passed away, so now it's my responsibility. Well, mine and my sister's."

"But many people travel and still have responsibilities back home."

"True. I guess I've just never been somebody who had that desire to travel a lot. I mean, there are some places I'd like to see."

"Such as?"

"Ireland and Scotland mostly. That's where my genealogy says we're from, so it would be kind of cool to go back to my roots. I'm not big on flying on airplanes, though."

"I'm sure you've heard it's safer to fly in an airplane than ride in a car?"

"Yes, I've heard that, but it doesn't help," Mia said, rolling her eyes. "

"I just can't imagine living without getting to see places all over the world," Olivia said. "I mean, this place is beautiful, but don't you ever get tired of looking at it?"

Mia shook her head. "Absolutely not. We have four seasons here, and every one of them is beautiful. Whether those mountains are blue and green, or they're yellow and orange, the colors are magnificent. And then in winter time, we lose the colors, but they are replaced with beautiful white snow several times a season. This lake is a gorgeous shade of blue coming from all the mountain rivers. We have springs and creeks. We have rocky cliffs. We have the most beautiful overlooks you'll find anywhere.

So, no, I never get tired of looking at my beloved Blue Ridge Mountains."

Olivia was furiously writing in her notebook, which she had brought in place of her electronic tablet since they were going to be next to the water. Mia wondered if Olivia was a little scared of her.

"So, tell me more about your mother. What kind of woman was she?"

Mia smiled thinking about her momma. She thought about her every day, every time she cooked something or welcomed a new guest or looked at her niece, who was her spitting image.

"My momma was a saint on earth. People came from many states to stay here just so they could spend time with Charlene Carter. She had a way about her, a certain essence that I've never seen in anyone else."

"You make her sound like she's perfect."

"She was pretty perfect. I mean, she had her flaws, like anyone else."

"What flaws?"

"She could be hot tempered. Sometimes she was grumpy in the mornings. She had a hard time forgiving people who did wrong to her or to me."

"Those aren't terrible things."

Mia looked at her. "You expect me to say terrible things about my mother? Is that the angle you're going for in this article?"

Olivia put her pen down. "I think you have this

opinion that I am trying to do something bad here. I'm really just trying to write an article, Mia."

"I don't think that's true. You see, the whole time you've been here, you've been very critical of everything you've seen. And this is our livelihood, but it's also our home. My momma made this place what it is, and my sister and I are just trying to carry on her legacy."

"But what about your own legacy? Don't you have one that you'd like to leave for your... You don't have children, right?"

"No. I do not."

"Neither do I. It was never something I was interested in. I mean, who wants to change diapers and clean up after snotty nose kids all the time?"

Mia rolled her eyes. "I would love that. In fact, I'd like an entire house full of snotty nose kids."

"Really? Then why aren't you doing that instead of trying to live out your mother's legacy?"

"Excuse me?"

"Well, I mean, it just seems to me that maybe you're trying to live for your mother instead of for yourself."

"Look, I will not discuss my personal life with you. This article is supposed to be about the honey business, and you've yet to ask me any questions about that."

"That's because Kate answered all of my questions about that. It is her business, after all."

"It's *our* business."

"That's really not the way she tells the story."

"What is that supposed to mean?"

"The way she explained it to me was that the honey business was basically her idea, and that she runs it. That's why I am asking you about the B&B. Are you running it because it's your dream? Or are you running it because it was your mother's dream and you feel guilty that she died?"

Mia was stunned. First by what her sister might have said, but then by what this woman was asking her. How dare she! Mia stood up, using all of her strength not to push the woman straight into the lake. It had only been a passing idea before, but right now it was a realistic possibility.

"I'm going to go inside before I do or say something I regret. I think you've gotten all the information that you need from us to write an article. Now, you're just a guest who has overstayed her welcome. I think you should start packing your things."

She turned and started walking back toward the house. Olivia called after her.

"You're very sensitive, you know," she shouted.

Mia ignored her and walked back into the house.

CHAPTER 6

"You told her to leave? Are you insane?" Kate said, throwing her hands in the air as she paced back-and-forth in the office. She was trying her best to be quiet, but she really wanted to scream at her sister right now.

"She's gotten enough information from us, Kate. Now she's just being snide and snarky and..."

"I don't think you should use any extra words."

"Look, I know that you're upset about this, but don't you find it the least bit stressful that this woman is here when we also have Lana Blaze locked in a room down the hall?"

"It's not like we kidnapped her, Mia."

Mia sank down into a chair. "Momma would know how to handle this. I swear, I can't take this kind of stress."

Kate sat on the edge of the desk and looked at her sister. "Yeah, I know you miss Mom. But it's me and you now, and we can't compare everything that we do to what she would do."

Mia stared at her sister like she had grown a second head. "You don't know because you never knew her, but she's a hard act to follow. And I want to think that she's proud of me."

"You know she is. But this is *our* business now. Our B&B, and our honey business."

"Not to hear Olivia Steele tell it."

"What is that supposed to mean?"

"Well, one thing that she told me was that you said the honey business was all yours. I had no involvement, apparently." She sat back in her chair, her arms crossed over her tiny frame.

Kate's mouth dropped open. "That is not at all what I said. I told her it was my idea originally, but that we run that business together. I even talked about the festivals that we do."

"Well, she must not have taken notes on that part. So, yes, I got a little angry at her tone. And then she started picking at me and picking at Momma. I just couldn't take it anymore."

"Well, I think you should apologize."

Mia stood up. "Are you crazy?"

"We have to make this magazine article a good marketing piece for our businesses. If she goes off angry and writes some terrible hit piece, we will never see customers again."

Mia took a deep breath and blew it out slowly, like she was trying not to explode. "She was rude. I have nothing to apologize for, and the very fact that you think I should swallow my pride and do it makes me think you're not on my side at all."

"Your side? Why are we picking sides? I'm always on your side. You're my sister."

"Well, it sure doesn't feel like it right now," Mia said before walking out of the office.

* * *

TRAVIS STOOD on the edge of the rock and stared out over the canyon. He loved taking pictures here. In fact, he had often met newly engaged or married couples here for the perfect photo shoot. He didn't think that there was a better spot in the entire area to get the perfect picture.

"Getting any good shots?" Mia asked, as she walked up behind him. He had been so immersed in his work that he hadn't even heard her driving up.

"That golf cart is awfully quiet," he said, laughing. Travis had helped Mia find a used golf cart that someone had refurbished so that she could get around the mountain roads near the B&B a little easier. Of course, she didn't drive it all the way into town, but she could visit a neighbor or tend to other areas of the property as needed.

"It's pretty cool," she said. He walked over and pulled her into a big hug, kissing the top of her head as he often did.

"Are you okay?"

"Can I ask you something?"

"Of course."

"Do you think I'm boring?"

Travis let out a laugh, thinking she was joking. When she didn't crack a smile, he realized she wasn't.

"Of course I don't think you're boring. Where on earth would you get an idea like that?"

"That stupid reporter. I did an interview with her today, and she made me feel like the most boring person on earth."

He took her hand and led her over to a large rock, pulling her down onto his lap. He put his chin on her shoulder as they stared out over the mountain range.

"Tell me what happened."

"Basically, she said that I am trying to live out Momma's dreams and not my own. She said that I should travel because that's what interesting people do, I guess. And then she sort of poked fun at me for wanting to have kids. I think she stopped short of telling me I'm too old or something."

He squeezed his arms around her midsection and pressed his lips onto her neck. "That woman is an idiot."

"Maybe she has a point," she said, standing up and facing him.

"No, she doesn't. What has gotten into you?"

"I don't know. Maybe she's right. I've been stuck in the same place for my entire life. I'm living out dreams that my mother had, but maybe I've lost sight of what mine are."

"I don't think so, Mia. You love this place."

"I'm not thinking about leaving here. But why don't I travel? I want to see Ireland and Scotland. Why do I insist on depriving myself of things like that?"

"I didn't know you wanted to see those places. We can make a plan…"

"And I'm in my thirties. I don't have any kids or husband. I'm going to end up being some kind of strange old maid living at a B&B that nobody wants to visit."

"I think you're getting a little ahead of yourself…"

"No, I'm not. As much as I can't stand her, she's made me think. I'm not living my life, Travis. I'm just staying here, taking care of everybody else, but not myself. This isn't where I thought I'd be at this stage of my life."

"Mia, what are you saying?"

She sighed. "I have no idea. I guess I just have a lot to think about. I want to go places and do things. I want to say I lived a life. I don't want to spend my entire life working for something and then find out it doesn't even exist."

Travis was very confused. But he knew Mia was the type of person who needed time to process her thoughts, and pushing her at this moment would do more harm than good. So he kept quiet.

"I have to go. I told the reporter to pack her things and leave."

He couldn't help but laugh. "I bet that went over well."

"Not with Kate. She is firmly on the reporter's side."

"I doubt that's true."

Mia groaned loudly. "Nobody is listening to me today. I've got to go."

He walked after her, catching up to her as she slid behind the wheel of the golf cart. "Mia, I love you. And I'm always on your side. I'm just saying that your sister is too. She's just stressed because she wants this article to help the business."

"I know. I just feel like I'm getting lost in my own life. I'll talk to you later," she said as she turned the wheel and headed down the dirt road.

Travis looked down at his camera and wondered if he could give her the life she wanted just taking pictures. Then he looked at his watch, realizing it was two-thirty. He had a decision to make. Was he going to go meet up with Cooper and Sally about the land, or was he going to keep doing what he always did - taking pictures and living a quiet life.

After what Mia just said, he had a lot of questions bouncing around in his head.

EVIE SAT ON THE SOFA, bored out of her mind. She couldn't wait to get back to school tomorrow. That was something she never thought she'd hear herself say.

Her mom had gone into town to do some shopping, and she wasn't sure where her aunt Mia had gone. She seemed to be unsettled today, like something was really bothering her. Of course, it was probably the terrible reporter woman who was staying at the B&B.

Of course, she would love to be hanging out with Lana Blaze, but she had slipped out of the house to take a walk on some hiking trails and clear her mind. Evie had enjoyed their conversation over breakfast. They talked about everything from Lana's early days as a singer to the state of human rights across the world. It had been quite a deep conversation for a teenager and a singing superstar to have.

Evie hated when the B&B was so quiet. She much

preferred a lot of activity, and sometimes she worried they weren't having enough guests stay there regularly. What if that reporter wrote an article that made that even worse? It seemed like a distinct possibility. Evie wanted the B&B to be a part of their family until she was old and gray herself, so she had taken more of an interest in it.

She didn't know where the reporter was right now, and she honestly didn't care. As long as she didn't have to interact with that woman, all the better.

She looked down at her phone and saw a message from her mother. Apparently a new landscaping crew was coming soon to trim the hedges and cut the yard. Kate wanted her to make sure to give them the check that she had left for them on the kitchen table.

Just as she was drifting off to take a nap, she heard a truck pulling down the driveway. Sure enough, she saw the name of a landscaping company on the side of it. Someone walked up and knocked on the front door. Evie got herself up and onto her crutches, hobbling over to the door to open it.

"Can I help you?"

The man, probably a little older than her mother, stood there with a clipboard. "I'm looking for Kate?"

"I'm her daughter. She's actually not here, but are you the landscape guy?"

"I am. I brought a couple of helpers with me

today so we can trim these bushes out front. We'll come back tomorrow to cut the rest of the property."

"Fine by me," Evie said, just wanting to go sit back down. He handed her a business card and then turned to go get his equipment out of the truck. Just as she was about to go back into the house, she noticed one worker getting out of the truck. Kieran.

He looked at her and smiled slightly, lifting his hand to wave. And then he started walking toward her. Why was he so good looking?

"Hey. I didn't know you lived here."

"Yeah, my mom and aunt run this place. I didn't realize school was already out for the day."

"Yeah, it was an early release day. How's the ankle?" he asked, pointing.

She chuckled. "A little better today. But, I am still using crutches, so there's that..."

"Listen, I'm sorry again. I am such a klutz..."

"It's fine. No hard feelings."

"I don't think your boyfriend felt that way."

"My boyfriend? I don't have a boyfriend."

"Oh. I thought the guy that came to the nurse's office..."

"Dustin? No. We're just friends."

Kieran smiled. "Well, I better get to work before I get in trouble. My dad said I had to get a part-time job, and this was the best I could find."

"Don't let me get you fired, then." She turned around, walked into the house and shut the door

84

behind her, leaning against it. And she couldn't wipe the smile off her face. Kieran was outside trimming her hedges, and there was no way she was taking a nap now.

* * *

COOPER STOOD next to his truck, waiting for Sally to finish her phone call. He hoped that Travis would show up, but he wasn't sure if he would. After all, he had been very skeptical about the idea of them going into business together.

But Cooper knew it was the right thing for him, at least. Even though he hadn't told Kate about his plans, he felt sure she would understand if he just explained it the right way. One day, he hoped they would get married, although he knew that was still a way off. After coming out of an awful marriage, Kate had expressed that she was in no hurry to get married again. They both enjoyed their relationship just like it was, at least for now.

"Sorry about that. It was my son's school. Apparently I forgot to sign the permission slip for a field trip next week," Sally said, slipping her phone into her pocket.

"No problem. So, you've got a son? Hard to believe we are old enough to have kids, right?"

Sally laughed. "Sometimes I still feel young in my brain, but then my body reminds me otherwise."

Cooper laughed. "I've had that experience. Of course, I don't have any kids of my own."

"No? Do you not want any?"

"I am dating somebody who has a teenage daughter. I don't think she's going to want to go through that again, but who knows?"

"Well, for what it's worth, I bet you'd make a fantastic dad."

"Thanks. So, I guess we should get on with touring the property?"

"Absolutely. I have to tell you I'm so excited that you're thinking about buying this place. I've always thought somebody should turn it into something special, and I know you'd be just the person to do that with your adventurous attitude."

Cooper chuckled. "Yeah, I was a lot more adventurous in high school. But I do think we could make this into something really cool that would bring a lot of tourists to the area."

Just as they were about to start the tour of the property, Cooper heard a vehicle pulling up behind them. When he saw it was Travis, he almost let out an audible sigh of relief. While he could start the business himself, having a partner he could trust would make it a lot easier. Travis turned off his truck, jumped out and walked toward them.

"Well, as I live and breathe! Travis? I haven't seen you since graduation!" Sally walked over and gave him a big hug.

"It has been a long time! You haven't changed a bit. So good to see you."

"I didn't tell you that Travis might come because I wasn't sure if he would," Cooper said. "But I hope the fact that he's here means that he is receptive to my idea." He stared at Travis, hoping for an answer.

"I gave it some thought, and I'm definitely interested in pursuing this. Still not totally comfortable with not telling Mia, but I wanted to come and see more of the property."

"Okay, does somebody want to let me in on what's going on?" Sally asked.

"Sorry. I want Travis to be my partner in this business, and I wasn't sure if he'd say yes or no until he showed up here today."

Sally looked back and forth between them, a confused expression on her face. "I seem to remember that you guys didn't really like each other in high school?"

Travis laughed. "You remember correctly. I guess the years can change things."

"I guess so! Well, shall we begin the property tour?"

"Absolutely. We can't wait to see every part of it," Cooper said.

Cooper had borrowed the golf cart from the B&B so they would have an easier time navigating the trails through the property. When Kate asked why he needed it, he told her he was going to do some repairs on it.

"Why don't we start with the cabins? We have several, although some of them are in disrepair, but I know that your carpentry skills would easily be put to use, Cooper."

"I am definitely looking forward to that," he said, winking at Travis.

* * *

MIA WALKED out onto the patio and found Kate sitting there, sipping on her afternoon cup of coffee. She looked peaceful, but Mia was quite sure she was probably wound up in knots. That's how her sister was most of the time, constantly worried about something, fretting over what she could've done better.

Of course, right now Mia was feeling much the same. Embarrassed by how she acted earlier, she had been looking forward to seeing Kate so she could profusely apologize.

"Mind if I join you?"

"Sure," Kate said, still staring straight out into the yard.

"How was your day?"

"Oh, pretty much just doing damage control. I had lunch with Olivia Steele at the café and tried to apologize for my rambunctious little sister's behavior."

Mia chuckled under her breath. "Rambunctious little sister. I guess that's one way to put it. Look, I'm really sorry, Kate. I screwed things up big time."

"Ironically, Olivia had little problem with it. She is so much of a bulldog, I think she kind of appreciated that characteristic in you. So, I hope I kept her from writing something terrible about our business."

"Did she leave?"

"No. Actually, she was planning to leave tomorrow afternoon anyway, so she's somewhere around the property taking more pictures."

"I promise to be on my best behavior from now until she leaves. If I have to offer to wash her feet or give her a back massage, I'll do it."

Kate laughed. "As someone who's been on the receiving end of one of your massages, I would refrain from that. Your little hands feel like a guinea pig is giving me a massage."

Mia leaned over and slapped her on the arm. "I can't help it if I'm small!"

Before they knew it, they were laughing together again. Mia was so thankful that Kate had forgiven her, and that what she had done had not resulted in a really unpleasant situation.

"So, where is Lana?"

"Evie said she went for a walk on some of the trails earlier. I assume she slipped back into her room at some point. I know she's requested chicken and dumplings for dinner, so I guess we will sneak a bowl up to her as soon as Olivia goes to bed."

Mia nodded. "I wonder how long she's planning to stay. I mean, I don't have any problem with her being here because I know she'll pay for her days, but it just feels like we can't move about freely without possibly blowing her cover."

"I don't know how somebody gets into that situation. I mean she has all the money and fame in the world, and she's still not happy. How can you be living your dream while simultaneously being miserable?"

"I totally understand it."

Kate looked at her. "Well, that makes me sad. What do you mean?"

"Some things that Olivia was saying caused me to react because she has a point. I don't travel because I feel like I have an obligation to this place. Plus, I'm scared to fly, so I've just avoided it. And I haven't gotten married or had any kids, and those are two of my biggest dreams."

"You know that you and Travis will get married and have a bunch of kids. It's just timing."

"I have absolutely no idea whether I can have children. No woman does. And I'm getting older. And I've known Travis since we were kids. It's not like we just started dating."

"Wait. Are you saying that you want to marry Travis right now?"

Mia shrugged her shoulders. "Obviously he doesn't want that because he hasn't proposed. But I just feel like I'm spinning my wheels lately. I love this place, don't get me wrong. I'll be here until the day I die, but I'd like to see parts of the world. I'd like to leave Carter's Hollow sometimes. But mostly, I want to be a mom. I see you with Evie, and I ache. I guess Olivia, with all of her bluntness, just uncovered some stuff I didn't want to think about."

Kate leaned over and put her arm around Mia. "I know all of those things are going to happen for you, sis. You need to tell Travis how you feel. Maybe he's scared to propose because you haven't been back together that long. Perhaps he thinks you'll say no."

"It's possible. I don't know. I guess I'm just having a pity party today."

"It's not a pity party. You're just having feelings and expressing them, which is always a good thing. Of course, I never expected that Olivia would be the catalyst for that, but at least she's good for something," she said, laughing.

"I suppose so. Well, I better go get started on the chicken and dumplings. You know how much preparation that takes," Mia said, standing up and walking towards the sliding glass doors leading into the kitchen.

"Mia?"

"Yeah?"

"You know our mom is watching over you, and

she's going to be so happy to see that you're taking control of your life. She would never want you to just live her dream. She would want you to find yours."

"I know. Thanks."

CHAPTER 7

*E*vie carefully hobbled down the front steps, a glass of lemonade in her hand. She'd ditched the crutches and opted to just limp a bit, sick of how they made her armpits feel like they were bruised.

The truck from the landscaping company was still there, although she didn't see Kieran anywhere. Maybe he was on another part of the property. Just as she was about to give up hope and sit down on the steps to rest her ankle, she saw the bottoms of his work boots sticking out from the last shrub in the row on the left side of the house.

"Hey," she said. Startled, he popped his head up and looked at her.

"Oh, hey. I didn't know you were there. You're off your crutches?"

"Trying to build some strength and confidence," she said, smiling.

"I was just pulling some weeds I saw back here. No good cutting the hedges if we aren't going to get rid of these weeds. But I think we're about done."

"Good. I brought you some lemonade. I wasn't sure if you liked that sort of thing. If you don't, we have sweet tea…"

He stood up and smiled. "I love lemonade. Thanks."

She handed him the glass, their fingers touching for a brief second, sending a little electrical charge straight up her arm.

"Everything looks nice. I'm sure my mom will be happy with the job you've done. Where's your boss?"

"I don't know. I think he said he had another part of the property he wanted to look at, so he may have walked off for a bit. The other guy that was helping us is cutting the shrubs on the other side of the house." He took a long sip of the lemonade. "This is good. Did you make it yourself?"

"Oh, no. My aunt Mia makes the best lemonade. I don't even try. Although, one day I'd like to run this place with my mom and aunt, so I'm trying to learn as much as I can."

"So you want to stay here? In Carter's Hollow?"

"Yeah. I think so. I'm from Rhode Island, but I definitely like it down south."

He nodded his head. "This is the first place we've

lived that I actually like. I could see myself staying here, starting a family and all that."

She was shocked at hearing a boy his age talking about starting a family. That just wasn't something teenage boys normally talked about.

"So you said you moved here with your dad?"

"Yep. We've only been here for a couple of weeks."

"Where is your mom?"

"She died when I was in elementary school. Breast cancer."

"I'm so sorry. I shouldn't have even asked. My grandmother died of cancer recently. I never got to meet her."

"Sorry for your loss too. "

"How did you end up in Carter's Hollow?"

"My dad got a job at one of the orchards. He's been working in the farming industry my whole life."

"I love the orchards. I've only visited one, right outside of town. They had the best apples I've ever tasted."

"That's probably the one where my dad works. I'm still trying to get my bearings around here. And driving these mountain roads is crazy."

"Oh, you have a car?"

"Just an old beat up truck. We bought it when we moved to town so I would have a way to school. We live so far out that I couldn't walk, and the bus doesn't come down our road."

"Well, I guess I better get back inside. I have some schoolwork to catch up on for missing a day. Thankfully, my teachers are giving me some extra time."

"Can I ask you something?"

"Sure."

"Do you think it might be possible if we…"

"If we?"

"Well, to make up for almost killing you, I was wondering if I might take you out for lunch or dinner?"

She could hardly contain her smile, and her heart was going so fast that she was afraid it might just pop out of her chest and land at his feet.

"I think that would be cool. Maybe at the café on the square?"

"Sounds good. How about after school tomorrow? I could drive us there."

She nodded. "Okay. Just try not to run into me before we can get to the car."

Kieran laughed nervously. "I will do my very best."

* * *

If Olivia Steele was anything, it was determined. As she sat in front of her laptop in her room, she typed out the first paragraph of her article for the third time. Starting an article was always the hardest part of the whole process. She knew she had to hook people in those first few sentences, but sometimes she just couldn't get her creativity to cooperate.

It didn't help that she had yet another fight with her boyfriend, David, half an hour before. Their relationship was obviously going down the tubes, but she didn't want to break up over text or phone when she was thousands of miles away. He was just another in a long string of men who couldn't live up to her standards.

Or maybe it was that she was so difficult to get along with. Even her mom had told her that over the years. But given the type of upbringing she'd had, strictly military, she had a hard time letting people in. After all, they'd lived in twelve different homes before she even got out of middle school. Olivia had never had an easy time making friends, but she had a very easy time of speaking her mind and being blunt about everything. It did not lend itself well to an intimate relationship with anyone.

She groaned as she deleted the first paragraph yet again. Working for a magazine such as this was proving to be difficult. Grits and Glory was supposed to be a down-home, sweet family style magazine that didn't have a bunch of talk about politics or religion or anything even remotely controversial. They filled the magazine with recipes and cheerful stories, and that was not something that Olivia was accustomed to.

But it was another steppingstone in her career, and she would do it with as much of a smile as she could muster. It paid well, and it allowed her to travel. Since she had never really wanted to have children, getting married was also something that she cared little about. Her career was the most important thing to her, and sometimes people tried to make her feel guilty for that. Just because she was a woman didn't necessarily mean that she had to be a wife or a mother.

She decided to shut her laptop and go outside for some fresh air. There was nothing about this article that was overly interesting to her, so she'd have to figure out a way to get it written, make her editor happy and get back to her normal life. Talking about a bed-and-breakfast out in the middle of the woods and a bunch of beehives wasn't exactly her idea of hard-hitting news. If only she could get that one big story that would change her career... It was something she thought about every single day.

She walked out of her room, shutting the door behind her. But when she turned to head toward the stairs, she ran into someone she never expected to see in her life, much less in the bed-and-breakfast where she was staying.

"Oh, my gosh. Are you Lana Blaze?" Even though

she knew the answer to the question, she still asked it.

"I… Um…"

"What are you doing here in Carter's Hollow?"

Lana stood there, staring like she didn't know what to say. "I used to come here when I was a kid…"

"Wait a minute. Didn't you get married at a place like this? Is this where you got married? I remember seeing it in People magazine."

"Yes, it was here." She sighed, like she was desperate to go anywhere else but here.

"I'm a reporter. Olivia Steele," she said, reaching out to shake her hand. Lana slowly lifted her hand.

"I know."

"So you knew I was here? Were you hiding from me?"

"Look, I might be a celebrity, but I have a right to my privacy. Now if you'll excuse me," she said, walking around Olivia.

"You know, being a celebrity doesn't entitle you to privacy. Your entire life is based on the public loving you."

Lana groaned and walked into her room. Now, Carter's Hollow was a lot more interesting than Olivia thought it was. There was no way she was leaving without an exclusive interview because it could totally change her career.

* * *

KATE PACED BACK-AND-FORTH in the kitchen, her blood pressure feeling like it was going through the roof. "I'm sure there is something we can do to come to a compromise here."

Olivia shrugged her shoulders and shook her head. "The only compromise I'm willing to come to is that I get a sit-down interview with Lana. I will not give up this opportunity that's sitting right in front of me."

Lana groaned. "Look, just because I'm a famous person does not mean that I have to give in to every interview request. I came here for a getaway. I don't want to do any kind of interview."

"I understand what you're saying, Lana, but I would be remiss in my duties as a journalist to not push back a little on that. I came here to do a sweet little interview about a B&B and a honey business, and I find the world's most famous singing superstar is living right next door to me. I can't just let that go." Olivia took a long sip of her wine and set it back on the counter.

"I don't see how this is a negotiation. She said no," Mia said.

"Okay, I didn't want to have to play this card, but you realize I can either write a nice article about your little business or I can tell the truth."

Kate almost lunged at her. "Are you trying to blackmail us?"

"Of course not. That would be illegal. I'm just letting you know I haven't decided which way to slant the story yet."

"You're not supposed to slant stories. You said it yourself. You're a journalist. Aren't you supposed to be objective?" Mia asked, her face turning a shade of red that Kate hadn't seen before.

"There are many angles to the story. I could talk about the inspiration of your mother and this bed-and-breakfast and how you started the honey business out of nothing. Or I could also write about the fact that one owner is trying to live her mother's dream and not her own life and how she was incredibly rude to me and maybe I couldn't make the recommendation of people staying here…"

"What kind of person are you?" Lana said. "These are the nicest people you'll ever meet in your life. And you're trying to bully them?"

"That's not at all what I'm trying to do. I'm just saying that the story could go one of two ways. It just depends on how I'm feeling in the moment," Olivia said, a snide look on her face.

"Fine. I'll think about it. But let me talk to Mia and Kate alone before I come give you my answer."

Olivia looked at Lana for a moment before answering. "Okay. I can't see where there's any harm in that."

"Thank you for your consideration," Lana said, sarcastically. Olivia got up from the table and walked upstairs, glaring at everyone as she went.

"I'm so sorry. I thought we were protecting you," Mia said, rubbing her forehead.

"It's fine. I've dealt with worse than her. And, she thinks we're going to have an interview, which is kind of funny."

"You're not going to do an interview?" Kate asked.

"Of course not. I wouldn't let that shrew interview me for anything. I might be a little down and out right now, but I'm not stupid. I know how to deal with somebody like her. Don't you worry." Lana leaned back in her chair and smiled. It was one of the first smiles they'd seen since she had gotten there.

"What are you going to do?"

"Let's just say that my celebrity status comes along with a lot of contacts, especially in the media. I just need to make a phone call, if you guys can excuse me for a moment?"

"Absolutely," Kate said as Lana walked out onto the back deck and closed the door behind her.

"Why are our lives so incredibly complicated right now?" Mia said, laying her head on the kitchen table.

"What's going on in here?" Evie asked as she

came down the stairs. "I can hear everybody talking really loudly all the way to my bedroom."

"In a nutshell, our lives are over." Kate laid her head on the table.

"Yikes. Seems like there's a lot going on down here I didn't know about."

"We've been keeping a secret," Mia said.

"Oh, you mean about Lana Blaze staying down the hall from me?"

"You knew about that?" Kate asked.

"We ran into each other in the hallway. Ended up having a nice breakfast together in my room. We discussed world issues and also some dirt on a few Hollywood types. It was cool."

"I guess we weren't keeping the secret very well after all," Mia said, looking at Kate.

"Is somebody going to tell me what's going on?"

"Basically, Olivia ran into Lana in the hallway. And she is trying to extort us to get an interview with Lana. Either Lana submits to the interview, or Olivia is going to write a terrible piece about us."

"Are you kidding me? She can't do that!"

"You're absolutely right. She can't do that," Lana said, breezing back in through the back door. She was grinning from ear to ear.

"What was that about?" Evie asked.

"I just spoke to the editor of Grits And Glory magazine."

"You did?" Kate said, her eyes wide.

"We don't have to worry about Olivia anymore. In fact, right now she's probably getting a phone call she wasn't expecting. Her employment with the magazine has now been terminated."

Mia and Kate smiled, both of them covering their mouths. "Should we feel bad that we got her fired?" Mia asked.

Lana laughed. "You should never feel bad getting a jerk like that fired. Besides, I did it, not you. She's getting what's coming to her. And she shouldn't work as a journalist anywhere, so she's probably going to be blacklisted when this is over."

"How do we keep her from writing something online or giving the story to another media outlet?" Kate asked.

"Her contract prohibits that, and she'll have to sign something saying she won't do that before she gets her last paycheck."

"But I guess that means we don't get an article in the magazine," Kate said, feeling a bit sad.

"That's the best part," Lana said, smiling.

"What do you mean?"

"Well, not only will you have a feature in the magazine, but the editor is going to allow *me* to be the one to write it. It's going to be a cover story!"

"You're going to write it? I didn't know you were a writer," Evie said.

"I'm pretty good at it, if I say so myself. And because I am the writer, it's going to be a tremendous marketing opportunity for the magazine. I can talk about my history of staying here as a kid, give all kinds of insight on your mother and talk about the honey business. It's going to be awesome!"

Kate couldn't contain herself anymore as she ran over and hugged Lana around the neck. Lana seemed surprised for a moment, but leaned into it.

"Thank you so much for saving this for us!"

"It's my pleasure. Now, if you'll excuse me, I need to go up and make sure that your guest has been notified that she no longer needs to worry about writing for Grits And Glory magazine."

As Lana walked up the stairs, Kate couldn't believe what had just happened. Not only would they get their magazine article, but it would be better than they had ever expected.

* * *

"So, Lana is writing the article for you?" Cooper asked, amazed.

"I know. It was totally unexpected. She's going to be staying on with us for at least another week or so. And the magazine will not promote the article until she's ready for everyone to know where she's been. That way she can stay here and nobody will blow her cover."

"And did Olivia leave?"

"Yes. She left early this morning, and she was not

happy with us at all. I think she might've been more relieved than she was letting on, though."

"Relieved?"

"She didn't like that job. She wanted something much more hard-hitting, so hopefully she can get on with a newspaper that will put her in the middle of a war zone or something. She'd probably love that!"

Cooper laughed. "I'm glad everything is working out. How did Mia take the whole situation?"

"She was stressed out like I was. But Mia's got some other things going on."

"What do you mean?" Cooper asked, picking up his sandwich. They had met at the café for lunch, something they hadn't gotten to do for over a week.

"I shouldn't say anything, but she's just really struggling with finding her own identity. She's been working so hard to preserve our mother's legacy that she hasn't started thinking about her own. I think she really wants to get married and settle down, start having kids, that kind of thing. And I want that for her. I have Evie, and I can't imagine not having her. Mia would make the best mother."

"What do you think is holding her up?"

"Well, mainly that Travis hasn't proposed. I don't understand it because they've basically been together since they were kids. What's he waiting for?"

Cooper shrugged his shoulders. "I don't know.

Maybe he just wants to build something to support his future family before he takes that step."

"I don't know why people do that. Nothing is ever going to be perfect. He just needs to take the chance. Mia is ready, and they can build a future together."

"Is that how you feel?"

"How I feel about what?"

"Are you thinking about getting married?" Cooper asked, nervously.

Kate smiled and reached across, squeezing his hand. "I would marry you in a heartbeat, but I'm in no rush. We haven't been together that long, and I'm enjoying the journey of getting to know each other."

"Good. That's how I feel. I just didn't want you to think I wasn't interested in building a future with you, Kate."

"Ditto." She took a sip of her tea and then turned to see something she hadn't expected. Her daughter walked in, more like stumbled in on her still sprained ankle, with a very tall and handsome boy.

"There's Evie," Cooper said.

"Yes, and she's with a boy that isn't Dustin." They crouched behind the menus that were still on the table.

"Why are we hiding?"

"Because I'm not ready for her to see me yet. I want to spy on this little date, and make sure this boy is a gentleman," Kate said, laughing.

CHAPTER 8

*E*vie had never been more nervous in her life. Sure, she'd been interested in boys before, even Dustin at one point, but this was something different. This was an extremely good-looking guy who had actually asked her to lunch. She didn't know what to do with herself.

"After you," he said, pulling out her chair. No boy had ever pulled out a chair for her. It must've been something about the south. She liked all the chivalry she'd seen, from men opening doors to giving up their seats when she and her mom were waiting for a table at a local steakhouse. It was just different here. There was a lot of yes ma'am and no ma'am, which had been hard for her mother to get used to. She thought people were saying that she was old, but Evie knew it was just a form of manners for southern people.

"Thanks," she said as she sat down. Kieran helped her push in her chair a bit and then sat across from her.

"I hope you didn't think that was dorky or anything. My dad always taught me to pull out the chair for a lady."

He had the bluest eyes she'd ever seen. When people said they could get lost in someone's eyes, she never understood what that meant until right now. She could've stared at them forever. It looked like little pools of ocean water dancing in his head. Staring at him probably wasn't her best move, or he might think she was some kind of weirdo.

"I think it was nice," she said, struggling not to blush. Since learning more about her family heritage, it made sense, but she turned so red faced when she got embarrassed. There was a ton of Irish and Scottish ancestry in her bloodline. Mia had even told her about a family castle in Scotland that they could visit. She hoped to do that one day.

"Good," he said, nervously looking down at his menu. It was obvious he hadn't done this a lot before. It wasn't like he came off as a player or anything.

"So, what are you planning to get?"

"I'm not sure. I've actually never been here before. Anything you can recommend?"

She surveyed the menu for a moment. "Well, my mom loves the chicken salad croissant. I've gotten the grilled chicken with fries before. Oh, and they have good fried catfish, if you like that sort of thing."

He smiled. "I love catfish, actually. Maybe I'll give that a try."

"What can I get y'all?" the server asked as she walked up. She was an older woman, probably getting near retirement age, with frizzy red hair and way more makeup than was necessary.

"You first," Kieran said, winking. *Oh, my goodness. He winked at her. That had to mean something. Or maybe he just felt bad for injuring her?*

"I'll have the chicken salad croissant with chips and a sweet tea, please."

"And you, young fella?"

"I'll take the catfish with fries, and sweet tea as well." He took Evie's menu and handed them both to the server.

Evie had to laugh when she heard people order sweet tea. It was pretty much a foregone conclusion that ninety percent of people in the restaurant were going to order that in the south. Occasionally she'd hear somebody say they wanted a particular soda, but rarely did anyone say they wanted unsweetened tea. It was like sacrilege.

As they sat there talking about school and things to do around Carter's Hollow, Evie found herself at ease with him. She felt the same way hanging around with her friend, Dustin, but this was different. She felt safe, secure. She felt like she could talk about anything, and she could do it for hours. Of course, she didn't know if he felt the same way. Evie had never fallen in love before, and she didn't know if this was the beginning of that, but it sure gave her butterflies in her stomach that she didn't expect.

"So you and your mom moved here from Rhode Island, but what about your dad?"

Evie chuckled. "Well, that's kind of a long story, and it gets a little complicated. My parents divorced when I was younger, and my dad disappeared from my life for a long time. But he recently came back into my life along with his new wife and my two siblings."

"That's great that you have a relationship with him now. I mean, if that's what you want."

"I do. It's been good. We had some struggles, but things are so much better now."

They continued eating, Kieran even giving her a bite of his catfish at one point. It felt so comfortable. It felt so real. Of course, her mother would tell her she was only sixteen years old, and that this was just puppy love, if it was love at all. All she knew was that she didn't want to go home or anywhere else. She just wanted to continue sitting across from him, learning everything about him and even talking about nothing at all.

"So, this place is beautiful, of course. But you've been here longer than me. Where's the best view?"

Evie grinned widely. "I happen to think I have the

best view in the entire area."

"What do you mean?"

"I love to climb up into this tree at the edge of our property where you can see everything, the valley, the river. It's gorgeous there. My mom's boyfriend built me a platform in the tree, so I go there almost every day. In fact, I'm going to do my homework there later if I can figure out a way to climb it with my ankle."

"Do you need some help to get up there?" he asked, smiling. *Did his eyes actually twinkle?*

"I think that would be great," she said. Her heart skipped more beats than she had ever felt before, but she couldn't worry about that right now because Kieran was going to climb into her tree with her, and that was the best thing she'd heard in a long time.

TRAVIS STOOD in front of one of the cabins, tilting his head to the side and rubbing his chin. "Are you sure we're going to be able to pull this off? I mean, you've got holes in the roof, and those floors need to be refinished."

Cooper nodded his head. "None of that is a big deal. Plus, people are coming for an adventure, not a stay at a five-star hotel."

"Yeah, but think about how much money we're

going to have to spend on materials. And you know prices have gone up."

"Stop worrying, man. I've got tons of spare lumber at my house. Plus, I've got some contacts that can get me some reclaimed wood if we need it. There's always a way around these kinds of issues."

"And we're still closing on the property Monday?"

"Yes. The bank has already done all the paperwork, so we should be ready. I'm so thankful that Sally negotiated with us. For a minute, I was worried we couldn't afford this place."

"What about marketing? I mean, how are people going to know about us?" Travis asked, obviously worried.

"We're going to set up a website and social media. I'm sure that Kate or Mia could help us with that too. Or even Evie. She's a whiz kid with social media."

Travis walked over to a picnic table in front of the cabin and sat down. "This whole thing has kept me up a lot at night lately."

"You're overthinking it. Kate and Mia are going to be excited. They're going to love this idea."

"Then why couldn't we tell them before we did it?" Travis asked, looking at him.

"Because you know they would've tried to talk us out of making any rash decisions, and I wanted to jump on this while Sally was willing to negotiate with us."

"I've been thinking a lot about my future with Mia lately."

Cooper sat down across from him. "Oh, yeah?"

"I just can't tell where she's at. She seems distracted and a little moodier than normal. It's almost like she's mad at me, but not really."

Cooper sighed. "Okay, I feel like I need to tell you something, but it's really not my place to tell you..."

"What are you talking about?"

"Maybe I shouldn't."

"Look, if you don't want me to be completely distracted while we're trying to build this business, I would suggest that you tell me."

"Well, it's just that Kate told me that Mia is struggling a little right now. She feels like she's living her mother's legacy and not following her own dreams."

"Are you saying she doesn't want to be with me anymore? That being with me is not part of her dream?"

"No. Her dream is getting married and having kids, and I think she feels like time is running out. She may think that you don't want to marry her."

Travis's eyes opened wide. "That I don't want to marry her? That's all I've ever wanted!"

"Well, then it sounds like you need to make a move, man. What have you been waiting for?"

He stood up and walked over to the tree and leaned against it. "I guess I've just been waiting until everything is perfect, you know? We had so many ups and downs for so many years, but I was afraid to jump out there and possibly have her say no."

"But isn't it going to be amazing to tell her about this business? Then she'll know that you're really serious about building a future for her and your future family."

Travis nodded. "Maybe. If she doesn't kill me for doing this without telling her."

Cooper laughed. "That is a possibility, but let's try to look at the positive."

"Why don't we take a walk down to the river? We need to mark off those trees along the way to see how long we can make that zip line. Have you called the company to do that?"

Cooper stood up and followed him as they started walking down the pathway. "Yeah, I left them a message. We need to take a look and see if this part of the river looks like it's going to be a good place for people to do some fly-fishing too."

As they continued walking and talking, Cooper got more and more excited about the business. He knew this was going to be something big for the area, but more important than that, it would take the weight off of Kate and Mia having to make sure that the bed-and-breakfast and the honey business were successful. He believed in both of the businesses, but he wanted to contribute more than just the occasional handyman or building job.

He had already been working with Mr. Pope on building his house, but once that was over, it wasn't like he would continue making income from it. With the adventure center, he would make income all the time, and that was something that would support a family. He already thought of Kate and Evie as his family, but one day he wanted to make it official. Before he did that, he wanted to prove to them he was a man who could take care of his family, and this business was the first step to making that happen.

MIA SAT across from Lana at the patio table. They had chosen this location so they could talk about the bed-and-breakfast and the honey business, both of which were visible during their conversation.

She had to admit that she felt a lot more comfortable being interviewed by Lana than she did Olivia. Lana wasn't out to get her, for one thing. Being interviewed by Olivia felt like a rabid dog was about to attack her at any moment, and she certainly had her guard up.

"Keep in mind that I'm not totally a professional

at this, so I might ask some stupid questions. Or I may even ask some questions that are way too personal. You just punch me in the arm if I'm getting too much into your business."

Mia laughed. "I'll remember that. But you're rich, and I'm not, so please don't sue me if I leave a bruise."

"Okay, so my first question is why did your mother want to start this B&B?"

"Well, she always had wanted to do this. It was like her big dream. She loved talking to people and welcoming them into the B&B. She loved cooking. She was full of southern hospitality, and all of this just came so naturally to her."

"What about you? Do you think you feel the same way about cooking and welcoming people as she did?"

She thought for a moment. "I guess so. I don't love it like she did. I mean, I enjoy talking to people, but I'm also much more quiet by nature than she was. And I'm not nearly as good of a cook. Wait. Maybe we shouldn't put that in the article."

"Don't worry, honey. I'm going to clean this up so that this place comes out looking like a diamond out in the middle of the forest, because it is. Some of my best childhood memories were here."

Mia was so thankful for Lana right now. "I mean, I love running the B&B. It's really interesting to meet people who come from all over the country, and we've even had a few people come from Canada and as far away as France."

"Somebody from France came to Carter's Hollow?"

"Yeah, we were surprised too," Mia said, laughing. "But there was just something about how my momma carried herself. People were just drawn to her, and they would tell their friends and family. I feel like some of that has died down since she passed away, and it makes me sad."

"Maybe it's because you need to put your own stamp on this. I mean, your mom can't be replaced, and trying to do things just how she did them... Well, maybe that's just not the right way."

"What do you mean?"

"I think there's a way to carry on her legacy without trying to be a carbon copy of her."

Mia felt a small stab at her heart. Not because she was mad at Lana for stating the obvious, but because maybe Olivia had been right about that part of it. She had been twisting herself in knots since her mother had died trying to live up to some imaginary expectations.

"I guess I have sort of lost who I am. You know, most women are wives or mothers. I'm just Mia. I'm just Charlene's daughter who's trying to hold it together. I am Kate's sister. I'm Evie's aunt. I am

Travis's girlfriend. But I don't really know who *I* am anymore."

Now she felt like she was at a counseling session. She was almost embarrassed to make eye contact with Lana for fear that she would decide she didn't want to write the article because Mia had too many emotional problems.

"I totally understand what you mean."

Mia was shocked. "Really?"

Lana laughed. "I'm sure it hasn't escaped your notice that I snuck onto your property in the middle of the night after driving all the way across the country just to get away from my life. Don't you wonder about that?"

"Yeah, we've kind of been wondering, but we didn't want to pry."

Lana put her pad of paper in her lap and laid down the pen. She leaned back and looked up at the sky. "Do you know how beautiful the sky is around here? I mean, look at that color blue. Not a cloud up there today. Do you know the last time I even had a moment to stop what I was doing and stare up at the sky like a kid?"

"I imagine you don't have a lot of free time given your touring schedule."

"I never have time to just take a breath. And I feel terrible complaining about it because I'm certainly financially blessed. I have more money than I could ever possibly spend if I stopped working right now. But, I miss being a regular person sometimes."

"I can understand that to some extent."

"What I'm saying is that we have a similar problem. You're playing the role of your mother, and I'm playing the role of Lana Blaze. You know that's not my real name?"

"Really? I guess I never looked it up, but I thought your parents must've been really cool."

Lana chuckled. "No. My parents were definitely not cool. My given name is Francis Tomlin. Not exactly the name of a singing superstar who wears fishnet stockings and leather miniskirts on stage."

"So what are you going to do?"

"I don't know. I feel trapped. There are contracts and plans for years into the future. But I've lost myself in all of this. I have money, but no love or happiness. I have a soon-to-be ex-husband who was just trying to use me as a stepping stone, and I honestly didn't care. But most of all, I miss doing the kind of music that I love. When I first started out, I was writing my own songs and singing in these little rinky-dink clubs or even on street corners. Now I pack the stadiums, which is great, but those aren't my songs. It's not even my style."

"Sounds like we both need to figure out who we are."

"Very true. So, who are you, Mia Carter?"

"I have no idea."

Lana shook her finger at Mia. "No, you're not getting off that easy. Close your eyes, take a deep breath and blow it out."

She did as she was told. "Okay."

"Now, you have your dream life. What does it look like?"

Mia started rattling off what she saw floating through her mind. "I run this B&B, but I'm married. I have two little kids who love to run around the house and get dirty in the lake. I volunteer at their school, and once a year we go on a big family trip somewhere. Last year we went to Scotland as a family and explored the beautiful green hills and the culture..."

When she opened her eyes, Lana was grinning from ear to ear. "Wow. That was magical. I felt you took me on a trip."

Mia's eyes welled with tears unexpectedly. "I don't know what that was. It felt so real."

"That was you visualizing your perfect future. So you need to go for it. Don't be like me and get caught up trying to please everybody else, Mia. It's a losing game."

She wiped away the stray tear that had escaped her eye. "Thank you, Lana. Truly. It really opened my eyes."

"You're more than welcome. I guess I need to do a little visualizing myself. Figure out what I want to do with my life."

"You deserve it."

"I guess we'd better get on with this interview," Lana said, picking up her notebook again. "Tell me what you thought when Kate came to you with the idea for the honey business…"

"Well, I thought she was nuts."

CHAPTER 9

"So, this is the infamous tree?"

Evie looked up at Kieran. "I need your help getting up there for sure. I don't see how my ankle is going to allow it."

"No worries. I am what my grandmother calls a 'strapping young man', so I should be able to help," he said, laughing.

She began her climb up the tree with Kieran bracing her from behind. He was carefully placing his hands on the backs of her legs rather than her rear end, which would've probably gotten uncomfortable really quickly. Within a few seconds, Evie was surprised to find herself sitting up on the platform like normal. She had missed sitting up in her perch the last couple of days.

A couple of seconds later, he was sitting beside

her. He looked around, smiling. "You're right, this is an amazing view."

"Right?"

"I can see the river over there. And look at those cliffs," he said, stretching out his long arm and pointing.

"I love coming up here. Unless it's storming or something, you'll find me up in this tree almost every day after school. I just think better up here."

They both leaned against the trunk and sighed simultaneously. "It's very relaxing. And I love this platform."

"Thanks. I mean, I didn't build it or anything. Cooper is very handy."

"So, you said he dates your mom?"

"Yeah. They've been going out for a while now. I assume at some point they'll get married."

"How do you feel about that?"

She smiled. "I would love it. I adore Cooper. He's funny, he's kind, and he can build anything. And he treats my mom nice, which is the most important thing. My dad wasn't so good at that."

He nodded. "I think it's great when people get second chances. It sounds like your mom got one."

"Did your dad ever remarry?"

"Yeah, unfortunately. I had a terrible stepmom for a couple of years, but she took off with some guy. Broke my dad's heart. It was awful."

"Sorry to hear that."

"That's one reason we moved here. She worked at the same farm as my dad, and it just made more sense to start over somewhere new. But I hope he finds somebody one day who treats him right. He's a hard worker, and he deserves a lot more happiness in his life."

She was finding Kieran to be a deep person. She'd never met any teenage boy who could have these kinds of conversations. He seemed very comfortable with himself and his feelings.

"Hey, I was wondering why you weren't here right after school…" Dustin said, poking his head up as he climbed up to the platform. He stopped speaking when he saw Kieran sitting on the other side of Evie.

"Oh, hey, Dustin. You remember Kieran?"

Dustin's facial expression faded, and he looked like someone had just punched him in the gut. "Oh yeah, I remember. What is he doing up here?"

"We had a late lunch at the café after school, and I needed some help to get up here with my ankle."

Dustin finished climbing and sat down across from them. "I could've helped you."

"Kieran was here. I didn't see a reason to call you to help me into the tree when he could."

"Look, man, we're just hanging out. It's no big deal."

Dustin glared at him. "May I remind you she can't climb this tree because of you? If you hadn't knocked your big gangly body into her, she wouldn't have a sprained ankle."

"Dustin! Stop acting like this!"

"Seriously? You're going to choose him over me?"

Evie was dumbfounded. Dustin had never acted this way. In fact, she'd never even seen him get angry, but right now he looked positively livid.

"I don't even know what you're talking about. I'm not allowed to have more than one friend?" Of course, Evie knew that her plans for Kieran wasn't about just being friends. She was hoping they might have some kind of relationship blooming.

"I've got to go," Dustin said, his face red. He climbed quickly down the tree and then ran up the trail before Evie could even say anything.

"I'm sorry about that. I didn't mean to upset him..."

"It's not you. I don't know what that was about. He's never acted that way before."

Kieran scrunched up his face. "I think he might be in love with you or something."

She let out a laugh. "No. That's not it. We've never acted that way with each other. We're just friends. He was the first person I met when I moved here."

"I don't know. It just seems to me he's interested in more than friendship. What do you think about that?"

"I think that he's just my friend, and that's what

he'll always be. I'll talk to him. I'm sure we can work this out."

"Do you think there's a possibility you and I might ever be more than friends?" he asked, barely making eye contact.

"Is that what you'd like?"

"I think so. You seem really cool, and I'd like to see where this goes."

"Kieran, are you asking me to date you?"

He nodded his head. "I think I am."

Evie grinned, again turning all shades of red. This was turning out to be a really awesome day.

* * *

IT HAD BEEN MORE than a week since Cooper and Travis closed on the property. Somehow, they had managed to keep the secret from Kate and Mia. But it made Travis feel terrible. He hated keeping secrets, even if it was to surprise them with the amazing new business venture he and Cooper had undertaken.

Of course, soon it would be time to market the adventure retreat, and there would be no way to keep the secret then. Cooper promised it would only be another week or so before they would sit Kate and Mia down and tell them what was going on.

Still, it had been difficult to keep them in the dark. They were both trying to spend as much time working on the property as they could, and that had created some rifts in both of their relationships.

"I think we should have all the cabins ready by the end of the week," Cooper said, standing back and looking up at the roof of one of them. He had been working practically nonstop since they signed the papers, often going to see Kate for a few hours and then working well into the night in the cabins.

"And they should finish the zip line tomorrow. The county has to come in and do some inspections for health and safety."

"Right. Then, we need to work on the website. I think we should hire an outside company. As much as I know Kate or Evie could probably help, I don't want to put any extra stuff on their plates. Evie has school, and Kate is busy with the honey business. She got a big order yesterday. Some boutique hotel chain in Atlanta."

"That's great. And Mia, bless her heart, isn't the best with technology." They both laughed.

"I can't believe how much we've gotten done in the last couple of weeks. This place is really coming together."

"It is. But don't you think we should go ahead and tell them?"

Cooper shook his head. "Let's just give it one more week. I want this place to be shining before we bring them over here."

Travis had gone back-and-forth on the idea of a

business, but now he was more confident about it. He liked the idea and thought it really would be a good future opportunity for both of them and their girlfriends.

Of course, he had other things going on in his head after his conversation with Cooper about proposing to Mia. It wasn't something that he took lightly. He had wanted to marry Mia since they were young, and that feeling had only grown since they got back together. But he wanted to make it the most memorable moment of her life, and every idea he mulled over in his head didn't seem to be good enough.

"I put together some ideas for packages. We can have packages for just fishing, corporate packages, and I think we could even use it for bachelor parties. Of course, without all the strippers and so forth."

Travis nodded. "And without the alcohol. We definitely don't want that going on here."

"True. What about the decor in the cabins? They're pretty bare-bones right now."

"I think Kate and Mia can help us with that, but not unless we tell them," he said, pushing again.

Cooper slapped him on the shoulder. "They're going to be great about it. This is a good thing. Stop stressing so much. It's not good for you."

As Cooper walked off to work on something else, Travis wished he could be more like him. He seemed to be completely unbothered by the fact that their girlfriends could dump them for keeping such a big secret. Maybe he was being overly dramatic.

Travis figured he probably worried more because he'd already lost Mia once before. It was the biggest mistake of his life, and he didn't want to repeat it. But he worried she was going to be angry with him for keeping the secret and for making such a huge financial decision without her involvement, especially if he was serious about building a future with her.

After all these years, he knew her well. He knew how she thought and how she was probably going to react. He just hoped that he could keep in her good graces somehow.

* * *

"IT'S WEIRD. It just is. Something is going on," Kate said, her arms crossed as she stood in the kitchen.

"I agree. He's canceled on me twice this week. And we always have dinner together." Mia leaned against the kitchen counter, a cup of coffee in her hand.

"I asked him about it. I even questioned him yesterday on the phone about why he was avoiding me. He just said he was really busy with work, which might be true because I know he's building Mr. Pope's house."

"Yeah, but he's built things before. Why is he suddenly avoiding you?"

Kate shrugged her shoulders. "I have no idea. I trust Cooper so I don't think he's seeing someone else or anything. But I don't understand what's happening."

"I don't think he would ever cheat on you. And I know Travis wouldn't do that to me. But they're definitely keeping a secret of some kind, and they seem to be doing it together. It would be too coincidental for them to act like this at the same time."

"Are you ladies trying to figure out men?" Lana asked as she walked into the kitchen. She had stayed a little longer than they expected, but they were getting used to having her around.

"Yeah, and it's probably a losing proposition," Kate said, rolling her eyes.

"If there's one thing I've learned about men over the years, it's that they're pretty simple-minded. We are much more complicated creatures than they are."

"Maybe so, but we can't figure out what our men are doing. They've been avoiding us like the plague for the last couple of weeks. They're obviously up to something."

"Listen, Mia, you just have to let it play itself out. They'll get caught in whatever scheme they're involved in. They always do," Lana said, laughing.

"So what's going on with you? I know you said you wanted to talk to your attorney yesterday."

"I did. The divorce is coming along nicely and should be settled soon. Of course, he gets a payout, which is to be expected. I'm sure news of the breakup is already hitting the tabloids. "

Mia scrunched her nose. "It is. I saw it at the grocery store yesterday."

"I'll have to tell my side of the story at some point, whatever my handlers tell me I can say. But I had an important conversation with my attorney yesterday about the future of my career."

Kate and Mia sat down at the kitchen table, and Lana joined them. "So, what's the plan?"

"Turns out that there are some clauses in my contracts that may allow me to get out early. My current obligations are only for maybe the next six months, and then I'm going to have some freedom to do what I want. So, there's going to be some big changes coming."

"Do you know what you want to do?" Kate asked.

"Well, for one thing I want to change my style, write my own songs and do less touring. I'd like to find somebody who I love at some point and build a family before I get too old to do it. It's going to be difficult, and I'm sure I'll get some pushback from my fans, but I'm going to start living the life I want to live. I've made all the money that I need, and that should buy me some freedom."

Mia leaned over and squeezed her hand. "You

inspire me. I'm already thinking of some changes I want to make."

Kate tilted her head to the side. "You have? What kind of changes?"

Mia smiled. "Well, I've been talking to a travel agent about different destinations. And I also found this company that will help me get over my fear of flying using exposure therapy. I'll have to go into Atlanta a few times, but it sounded kind of cool."

"That's amazing, Mia," Lana said. She was one of the most encouraging people Mia had ever met.

"I'm proud of you, sis. I'm glad to see you opening your horizons."

"And, I'm also going to take up some hobbies. There's a yoga class in town that just started, so I think I'm going to sign up. And there's an art class where I can learn water colors and paint mountain landscapes. I think that might be fun. I'm just trying to keep my options open."

"I think that's awesome. You're going to do fine," Lana said, smiling. "In fact, I think we're all going to do fine. I think the next year of our lives is going to be amazing!"

Mia and Kate held up their coffee mugs. "Hear, hear!"

Lana looked at them. "This would be more impactful if you guys had actually poured me a cup of coffee." Kate and Mia laughed.

"You practically live here now. I think you can

pour your own cup of coffee," Mia said, leaning back in her chair with a sly smile.

* * *

EVIE SAT NERVOUSLY UP in her tree. It had been a couple of weeks since Dustin had spoken to her. She really didn't understand what was going on with him. They had never talked about dating, and she wasn't sure if he had gotten the wrong idea somewhere along the way.

At the same time, she was having some of the happiest times of her life dating Kieran. She had introduced him to her mother and her aunt, and he'd come over for dinner a couple of times and had even helped with some of the beekeeping duties once Kate had taught him a few things. He had really woven himself into the fabric of her family quickly.

Since he was her first actual boyfriend, she wasn't quite sure how she felt about that. What if things didn't work out, and her family got mad at her if they broke up? These were the types of things that sometimes went through her mind, but for the most part it had been smooth sailing. They had gone out on many dates, to the movies, mini golf and even on a picnic overlooking the mountains.

But it bothered her that her friendship with Dustin had seemed to fall apart so easily. And since he wouldn't speak to her, she didn't really know how to fix it. So, in a final desperate attempt to get him to talk to her, she had slipped a note into his locker asking him to meet her at the tree at three o'clock. She told him if he didn't show up, she would consider their friendship over since he apparently didn't want to speak to her.

She had also told Kieran what she planned to do because he knew how important it was for her to have a friendship with Dustin. Thankfully, he understood and didn't seem to be the jealous type.

But now it was five minutes after three, and there was no sign of Dustin. She had homework to do, so she turned to pick up her backpack so she could head down the driveway and back home since it was apparent that he wasn't coming. Just as she leaned over to start climbing down, she saw him appear from out of the woods.

He stood there for a moment, not walking any closer, hands in his pockets. There was no expression on his face. No hatred or look of friendship. Just nothing. Finally, his feet started moving again as he walked over to the tree. She scooted back, giving him room to climb up and sit next to her, which he did.

For a few moments, he didn't look at her. In fact, he was completely quiet, and she didn't know what to say.

"I'm glad you came," she finally said, quietly. He cleared his throat. "

"I wasn't sure that I was going to come."

"Dustin, I don't understand what happened."

"That makes two of us."

"So, you stormed away from here, got mad at me and stopped speaking, but you don't know why?"

"That pretty much sums it up."

"Can I ask you something?"

"Yeah."

"Do you have... feelings for me or something?"

He looked at her and chuckled under his breath. "No, of course not."

She threw her hands up in exasperation. "Then I don't understand what's going on!"

He ran his hands through his thick hair. "I guess I was just afraid I was losing you as a friend."

"So you stopped speaking to me because you wanted us to still be friends? Do you realize how ridiculous that sounds?"

Dustin sighed and leaned his head against the tree. "You know you were my first really good friend here."

"What are you talking about? You had a huge group of friends that you knew before I ever even moved here."

He shook his head. "No. That's not true. I *know* a lot of people, and we hang out, but they aren't my true friends. They aren't my best friend."

"Are you saying I'm your best friend?" Evie asked, putting both of her hands over her heart.

He didn't make eye contact, and his head nodding was almost imperceptible. "I guess so."

"Then why are you pushing me away?"

"Look, I know how this goes. You get a boyfriend, and suddenly you start spending all of your time with him. Before you know it, we're just two people passing each other in the hallways at school."

"Well, when you stop speaking to me, you're pretty much making that happen anyway, aren't you?"

"I didn't say it made sense. But it felt like it was easier if I just took the lead and ended things before it got too painful."

"Dustin, I'm just dating him. I don't even know if it's going to work out. This is the first time I've even dated a guy seriously. But nobody is ever going to replace you. I think of you as my best friend too."

He finally looked up, a slight smile on his face. "You do?"

"Of course! You had me so confused. I thought maybe you had feelings for me in a different way."

He shook his head. "No. I thought I did when we first met, but then I realized that I would never want to risk our friendship. I guess I didn't think ahead to what would happen if you started dating somebody."

She reached over and squeezed his knee. "We are forever friends. No boy is going to get in the way of that. And if you start dating some girl, you better make sure she knows about me."

Dustin laughed. "You have yourself a deal."

She crawled over and gave him a hug. "Now, can you please stop being so mean to my boyfriend?"

CHAPTER 10

"*I* cannot believe we're doing this," Mia said, putting her hand over her forehead. They had been sitting on this deserted dirt road for well over an hour.

"Don't you want to know what's going on?" Kate asked, looking around in every direction.

"We're not exactly stealth. If they pull up here, they're going to see us."

"Well, then we'll confront them, won't we?"

Kate had been like a dog with a bone. She couldn't let go of the fact that Travis and Cooper seemed to be hiding something. So she had concocted the idea of driving over to Mr. Pope's property to see if Cooper was actually working there.

Sure enough, they had gotten there and there was

no work being done. Cooper wasn't there, his truck wasn't there, and the place seemed like a ghost town.

"You can clearly see he's been doing work over here at some point," Mia said.

"Yes, but he's supposed to be doing work right now. That's what he told me on the phone earlier. He couldn't have lunch with me because he was working on Mr. Pope's property and would be tied up with that all day. But you can see that he's not here. So where is he?"

Mia shrugged her shoulders. "I have no idea. Travis told me he was taking some pictures today, but there's no way for me to check that."

"I just don't get it. Both of them are the most honest people I know. Why would they suddenly start lying?"

"I don't know. But can we please go back to the B&B? This isn't getting us anywhere."

Begrudgingly, Kate nodded her head and started the car. As they were driving down the road, she thought about why this was bothering her so badly. Maybe it was because she had been burned in the past with Brandon, her ex-husband. She didn't think Cooper would cheat on her, but then again, she didn't think Brandon would betray her either.

"Let's go back a different way than we came. I don't want to hit that hole in the dirt road again."

"But it's going to take us a good extra ten minutes going that way," Mia complained.

"You'll be fine," Kate said, rolling her eyes.

When they got down to the area where they were going to turn, Kate saw something out of the corner of her eye. "Is that Travis's truck over there?"

Mia leaned over and looked out the window. "I think so. Yeah, that definitely looks like his truck."

They looked at each other, obviously sure of what they were about to do. Kate turned the wheel toward Travis's truck and eased her car into a spot as quietly as she could.

"Is he in the truck?" Mia asked, trying to look into the tall cab.

Kate was able to get a better view. "No. And I think I see Cooper's truck down there," she said, pointing down the gravel driveway.

"What would they be doing over here? And why are they together?"

"They are definitely up to something, sis. And I think it's time we find out what it is. Come on," Kate said, opening her car door and quietly closing it. Mia followed.

They slowly walked down the gravel pathway. The first thing Kate saw were some little cabins that she had never known were there. She could also see the river off in the distance and what appeared to be a zip line.

"What is this place?" Mia asked.

"Well, I don't know. You've lived here your entire life. I was hoping you could tell me."

"I've never seen any of this. I didn't know there was a zip line in Carter's Hollow."

"Let's see if we can find them."

They kept walking until they came to the first of the cabins. There was no sound, and all they could hear was the river that was getting closer with every step.

Then Kate thought she heard Cooper talking. He had a loud, booming voice, and it was echoing around the valley.

She put her finger to her lips to tell Mia not to make any noise, and they crept over to the third cabin, where it sounded like Cooper was talking. They stepped up onto the porch and pushed the front door open to find Cooper and Travis sitting at a makeshift table eating lunch. The looks on their faces were priceless.

"Kate? What are you doing here?" Cooper said, his eyes wide and his mouth hanging open. He looked like a kid whose hand had been caught in the cookie jar.

"I think the better question is, what are you doing here? You're supposed to be working on Mr. Pope's property today. Isn't that what you told me?"

"I... Well..."

"And you, Travis, told me you were going to be taking pictures today. Where is your camera?"

Travis looked down at the table, even though he obviously knew his camera wasn't there.

"Listen, Mia... We can explain..."

"You guys have been lying to us about something. And we want to know what it is, right now," Kate said, sternly.

"It's nothing bad, Kate" Cooper said, standing up, holding his hands up like he was about to brace for an attack.

"Any time you lie to the person you supposedly love, that's bad."

"I know. But I just didn't want you to think our idea was stupid or something."

"What idea are you talking about?" Mia asked, obviously frustrated.

"I came up with an idea, and I wanted Travis to go into business with me."

"Business? What kind of business?" Kate asked.

"Mr. Pope told me about this property, and I thought it would make a great adventure destination. Basically, people can come here, stay in one of the little cabins or even camp on the property. We would take them on guided fishing trips, sightseeing, hikes. We even had a zip line installed." Cooper stood there, a smile on his face as he proudly explained.

"Wait. Are you saying that you and Travis bought this property and started building an entire business without even talking to us about it?" Kate asked.

Travis and Cooper froze in place. It was like they

didn't know what to say, and Kate thought she could feel her blood actually boiling in her body.

"Are either of you going to answer?" Mia asked, her hands on her hips.

"Look, it's my fault. Don't get mad at Travis. I talked him into it."

"I'm pretty sure Travis is a grown man and can make his own decisions," Mia said, glaring at him.

"You're right. I decided on my own."

"Why on earth would you do something like this and not tell us?" Kate asked.

Cooper blew out a breath. "I was worried that if I told you, you would try to talk me out of it."

"So you just do something behind my back? Instead of being an honest person?"

He walked toward her. "Come on. You're busy with your businesses, and the reporter was here. I had an opportunity that I didn't want to miss out on, and I just grabbed it. I figured you'd understand..."

"Well, I don't understand. This is a big deal. It's going to change everything, and apparently you don't value my opinion."

He tried to walk closer, but she held up her hands. "I know you're mad. I hope when you've had some time to think..."

"Don't patronize me."

Mia continued staring at Travis like she didn't know what to say.

"Mia, I hope you're not too mad at me..."

She also held up her hands. "Mad at you? I'm very heartbroken that you didn't trust me enough to tell me what you were doing. What did you think? That I wouldn't support your dreams? Or that I just didn't have a right to ask questions?"

"I would never think that. Of course you have a right to ask questions."

"You know, I thought we were heading somewhere, Travis. I thought we had a future, maybe even as husband and wife. But I don't want to be with somebody who hides something so big from me. Kate, can we leave?"

Kate nodded her head, took her sister's arm and walked out of the cabin.

"Come on, y'all! Give us a chance to explain!" Cooper called to them as they quickly walked back up the gravel driveway. Neither of them turned around.

* * *

"Are you sure you have to leave?" Mia said, hugging Lana around the neck for the tenth time that day. She didn't know why she found herself so attached, but she did.

"I know. I hate that I'm having to leave, but I've got a show next weekend that I have to prepare for. My agent is ready to wring my neck."

"How do you feel about going back?" Kate asked.

"I'm actually kind of excited. I think things are really going to change for me, and I'm looking forward to having more control over who I am and what I do. I really needed this break. I needed time to think."

"Good. I'm glad you could take some time for yourself, and I look forward to what you're going to do in the future," Mia said, smiling. She really was happy for Lana, even though her own life seemed to be off the rails right now.

After the argument that she and her sister had had with Travis and Cooper a few days ago, Mia wondered if things were over with their relationship. He had tried to call her a couple of times and even texted a few days ago. Each time, Mia just didn't know what to say. She didn't know how to feel.

Kate was angry. There was no doubt about that. She was really upset at Cooper, but Mia knew they would end up right back together, eventually. Kate just had to cool down and realize that Cooper was just trying to build something for their future. He was a go-getter, a type A personality, much like her sister.

But for Mia, it felt like betrayal. It felt like Travis didn't trust her. She knew that wasn't true, but it still hurt and she didn't know what to do with that kind of pain.

"Well, I'd better be off. Don't want to miss my

plane. Thanks for having me here and getting me through this crazy time. I hope you guys work things out with your fellas. They are good men, and sometimes you have to look past the stupid things that they do."

Mia laughed. "Very true. I hope we can figure things out. Have a safe trip."

As they watched Lana walk down the front steps and get into her car, Mia was a little sad. She had enjoyed having Lana around, and it had almost felt like she had an extra sister. She hoped they would continue having a relationship, but she would understand if Lana was too busy with her celebrity life to keep up with two women who lived out in the mountains of Georgia.

"Well, I guess that's that. I have some book-keeping to do. What are your plans this afternoon?" Kate asked as she shut the door.

"I don't know. Listen, do you think we're doing the right thing? With the guys?"

"You mean by totally ignoring their existence on the planet?" Kate said, laughing under her breath.

"Yeah."

Kate sighed. "Probably not. I feel like some high school girl trying to punish her boyfriend. Something about it just doesn't feel right in my gut."

"Oh, thank God. I was afraid it was just me being a pushover or something. What do you think we should do?"

"Well, I think I should go talk to Cooper. It seems like he was the instigator of all of this, and I need to understand why he did it."

"That doesn't really help me with Travis. I don't know why it just makes me feel like he betrayed me in some way."

Kate rubbed her arm. "Because you have history. Cooper and I don't have a history like that. And - I mean this in the nicest possible way - you're a lot more sensitive than I am."

Mia laughed. "That's no secret. I just don't know how to get past him lying to me."

"Why don't you let me go talk to Cooper and see how that goes? Then you can decide on what to do with Travis. In the meantime, if you'd like to handle the bookkeeping, I will go find Cooper."

Mia nodded. "Okay, as long as you understand you'll have to check the numbers behind me because you know I'm not good at that sort of thing."

"I believe in you," Kate said, giggling as she grabbed her keys and walked out the front door.

* * *

TRAVIS PUT the last coat of paint on the picnic table. Cooper had come up with the crazy notion of painting them white so they would stand out and look clean against the backdrop of the cabins. What they found out was that painting picnic tables white in the middle of the woods was no easy task.

"I swear these look ridiculous," Travis said, slapping the paint brush down onto the table.

"Are you sure it's not that you're just really upset about this whole thing with Mia and Kate?"

Travis turned and glared at him. "You know what, I'm pretty mad with you, actually."

"Why are you mad at me?" Cooper asked, throwing his hands up in the air.

"Because I would've told her immediately. You were the one that said we should keep it a secret, and I knew I shouldn't have listened to you. You had bad ideas back in high school, and you have bad ideas right now!"

"Are you kidding me? You could've said no. You could've told me you were going to tell Mia whether I liked it or not. You do have a mouth, don't you?"

"Seriously? You would've flipped your lid and it would've been a whole thing, and I didn't want to deal with it."

"Wow. I've seen women have a catfight, but I don't think I've ever seen men do it," Cooper turned around to see Kate standing there watching them.

"Kate?"

"That's me."

"I think I'm going to go wash these paint brushes off. Excuse me," Travis said, picking up the paintbrush and disappearing down to the river with a bucket in his hand.

Cooper walked closer. "I have to say that I'm shocked to see you here."

"I'm shocked to be standing here."

"So why are you?"

"Because I want to give you a chance to explain while I'm calm. I think I just needed some time to process what happened, and I don't really know how to feel right now. But most of all, it's affecting Mia, and I don't want her to feel like this anymore."

Cooper pointed at one of the unpainted picnic tables, inviting her to sit down with him. She slowly walked over and sat down, placing her hands on the table like they were about to embark upon a serious business meeting.

"Kate, first of all I want you to know that I did this for us. For our future."

"Maybe that's what you thought you were doing, but to hide something as big as this, a huge time and money investment, I just don't understand why you couldn't tell me."

He sat there for a moment and then blew out the breath that he'd been holding. "Ever since I was a kid, I've wanted to be something. To really be the boss of my own company or do something that other people could look up to. And I find myself just doing handyman jobs all over this area, never really getting anywhere. Constantly spinning my wheels. And looking to have a future with you and Evie, but never feeling like I am financially stable enough to do it."

"I never asked you to do anything different from what you were doing, Cooper. You're highly talented at carpentry, and I was so proud when you got the job building Mr. Pope's house."

"I know that you're proud. And I'm grateful for that. But I wanted to be proud of myself. So when Mr. Pope told me that Sally was selling her family land, it gave me the opportunity to do something I had always wanted to do. This was an idea I had years ago. I was just too afraid to talk about it because it seemed like a pipe dream. I didn't want you to think I was some sort of head in the sky dreamer who would never do anything."

"I would never think that about you."

He smiled. "I know. But you see me in a totally different way than I see myself. Maybe it's a man thing, but I needed to prove to myself that I could do this with nobody else's help. Well, other than Travis. I knew I needed a partner, and he can't take pictures for the rest of his life. He's not making nearly enough money to support a family, and he wants a family with Mia."

"I'm sorry I didn't give you a chance to explain this much the other day. I was just so shocked that you had gone out and spent so much money on this land and planned a whole business without even talking to me about it."

"The truth is, we were going to tell both of you in another week. We just wanted to get some more things in place so that when we brought you out here, you would be impressed at what we had done. We knew you'd probably be aggravated, but I didn't expect the reaction that I got."

She reached across the table and put her hand on his, which made him feel light years better than he had a few minutes before. "I'm sorry for how I reacted. I should have known that you had a reason for doing what you did, but you have to promise me something."

"Anything."

"Promise me that in the future you will talk to me before you make such a big decision. I know we're not married, but I want to know that we can count on each other and trust each other for the small decisions and the big ones."

"I promise."

"And I'm very proud of what you've done. This is a great idea, and I can't wait to see how successful it is."

He stood up and took her hand, pulling her up close to him. "Thank you. Hearing that from you means more than you'll ever know."

She looked up and kissed him. "I do have a question."

"What's that?"

"You said that Travis did this because he wants to build a family with Mia?"

Cooper stilled for a minute. "I shouldn't have said that out loud."

Kate laughed. "But you did. Are you saying that Travis wants to get married?"

"Well, you didn't hear it from me, but yes. He really wants to marry Mia, but he was afraid he had nothing to offer with just his photography business. It's so unstable, and he wanted something that could provide financial stability for a growing family."

"So why isn't he proposing?"

"I think he's planning to at some point, but he's driving himself crazy trying to figure out the perfect way to do it."

"There is no perfect way. She just wants to get married and start a family with him. She doesn't care about the whole proposal thing nearly as much as she cares about just starting her life with him."

"Are y'all talking about me?" Travis asked, walking up the hill.

"Absolutely. Listen, we have some things we need to talk about," Kate said, pulling on his arm.

CHAPTER 11

Kate and Mia sat at the kitchen table, nervously looking at the unopened envelope. "You open it," Mia said, sliding it over to her sister.

"No. You open it."

They'd been doing this for the last five minutes, neither of them willing to actually open the package. Finally, Evie stepped in and ripped it open, tossing the magazine onto the table in front of them.

There was that month's new issue of Grits And Glory magazine with a picture of Lana on the front holding a jar of their honey. They both froze in place, staring at the image.

"Oh, my gosh. She's holding our honey. Do you know what a crazy thing that is? That's like free marketing. We can frame that and hang it right here in the kitchen," Kate said, her eyes wide as she looked at it.

"Aren't y'all going to read it?" Evie asked. Mia had to laugh inside of her own mind when she heard Evie use the word 'y'all'. She was finally turning into a southerner.

"Why don't you read it to us?" Kate said.

"Fine. But you're being ridiculous," Evie said, rolling her eyes. She picked up the magazine and found the page where the article started. She began reading the introduction, which was basically Lana explaining her childhood and how she had come to stay at the bed-and-breakfast and gotten to know Charlene. She then gave background on Kate starting the honey business and how Mia was continuing her mother's legacy by cooking all the wonderful food that her mom had cooked.

"It's a great article so far," Mia said, reaching across the table and squeezing Kate's hand. "I can't believe we're going to get this kind of national attention."

"Listen to this part," Evie said. "Going to Sweet Tea B&B is like being swept back in time. From the beauty of the mountain ranges that line the land-scape to the kindness of the people you'll meet, there is no place I've found in this great country that has made me feel more at home than Sweet Tea B&B. Kate and Mia become your sisters while you're there, and you'll never find better food. From comfort food like chicken and dumplings to the decadent chocolate cake that Mia brings out for special occasions, the food is worth the trip all by itself. But, most importantly, you'll feel the spirit of the woman who started it all, sweet Charlene who's name now adorns each jar of honey that's made right on the property."

"That's just beautiful," Mia said, dabbing at her eye.

"It really is. Lana did a wonderful job on the article."

"I think I'll run to the store and get some more copies of this. I want to make sure we've got plenty on hand to show to guests," Kate said.

As Mia sat in her mother's kitchen, holding the magazine in her hand, she thought about how hard her mother had worked to build this place so many years ago. She thought about all the guests who had come to stay over the years, all the food that had gone into all of those stomachs. She thought about meeting her sister and her niece. She thought about Travis showing up at the front door. She thought about the honeybees out back and the fish in the lake that her newly found dad had caught. There were so many memories surrounding Sweet Tea B&B that it was almost overwhelming to think about.

She hoped that her mother was proud of her,

wherever she was. But Mia had come to realize that she could preserve her mother's memory and legacy without sacrificing herself in the process. She could grow and do new things without giving up the old. She could be who she wanted to be without feeling like she was living in the shadow of some unattainable goal. She felt free.

"WHY ARE WE HERE?" Mia asked as they pulled up to the adventure center. Even though Kate and Cooper had mended fences, Mia had still not spoken to Travis. She just didn't know what to say. Part of her was still hurt, and part of her was embarrassed for not getting in contact. And he had stopped contacting her, which was even scarier. There was a good chance that their relationship was over.

"I promised Cooper that I'd come by, and I really didn't want to have to drive back over here again today. At least walk down there with me. See what they've done."

"I saw it already. I'll just wait in the car."

"No. You've got to face him sometime, Mia."

"What am I supposed to say if I see him?"

"Look, I don't even think you're going to see him. Cooper told me he was going into town today to sign some papers at the bank."

Mia looked at her quizzically. "What kind of papers at the bank? They already closed on this place."

"I don't know. What, are you writing a book? I'm just telling you what he told me. Maybe it was something they forgot to get them to sign."

"That literally makes no sense, but whatever."

"Just come on," Kate said, pressing her.

They both got out of the car and started walking down toward the cabins. Mia didn't know why she had to go with her to see Cooper. But she wanted to get back to the B&B as soon as possible, and it seemed like her sister just would not give up.

"Hey, babe," Cooper said as he walked up. "Hey, Mia."

"Hello," Mia said, still aggravated that Cooper had apparently started this whole situation. Although, she knew that the business idea was a sound one. When Kate had explained everything to her, she was actually pretty impressed at Cooper's idea. But that didn't mean she wasn't still hurt that Travis didn't tell her.

"Don't worry. Travis isn't here. He had to go into town."

"Why would I care?" she said, crossing her arms. She didn't actually mean it, of course. She did care. A lot.

"Listen, while you ladies are here, I was wondering if you might do me a favor?"

"What is it?" Kate asked.

"I need a couple of guinea pigs to try out the zip line."

Mia stared at him like he'd lost his mind. "Are you crazy? I don't even ride roller coasters, and you think I'm going to zip line through the forest? What if I fall off that thing and I end up being dinner for a bear or a bobcat?"

Cooper laughed. "I promise you're not going to fall off that zip line. Plus, it's an amazing view up there. You've never seen the mountains like this."

"And who's going to catch us on the other end?"

"We've hired a couple of workers. We've all been trained on zip line safety."

"I think it sounds kind of fun," Kate said. Mia found that awfully suspicious seeing as how Kate was not a risk taker either. They must've had that genetically in common.

"You'd really be doing me a favor," Cooper said, putting his hands in the prayer position.

"Oh, and I so want to do you a favor right now," Mia said, giving him a blank look.

"I know you're still mad at me, but I think a good whiz through the forest on a zip line is going to be just the thing for you to forgive me," Cooper said, grinning.

"Fine. If it will get me back to the B&B where I can make myself a nice pot of coffee, then I'll do it.

But if I die, I swear I'm going to haunt you until the end of your days!"

A few minutes later, Mia was standing on the platform watching her sister get hooked up. "Make sure you've got this thing all nice and tight," Kate said before giving Cooper a kiss.

Seconds later, she was screaming and flying through the forest. Mia wanted to run straight back to the car. This just wasn't her thing, and she wished she hadn't agreed to it. She had never been an adrenaline junkie, opting instead to sit on the sidelines while other people did things that could get them killed.

"Maybe I'll just go over here and wait at the picnic table," she said, inching her way backwards before Cooper took her arm.

"It's going to be fun. You're going to love it!"

"I highly doubt that."

Begrudgingly, she walked forward and allowed Cooper to put the harness on her. She checked every cable and strap at least three times before she stepped up to the end.

"I don't know why I'm doing this. I'm going to strangle you when I get back over here," she mumbled, but certainly loud enough that Cooper could hear her.

"I promise you that by the time you get to the other side, you're going to be thanking me. This is going to be a life-changing ride." With that, he gave her a quick push, and she was flying through the air.

The first few seconds were just complete fear. She heard a bloodcurdling scream and then realized it was her own voice. But then, something happened. Something magical. She was able to let go and start looking around. She took a deep breath of the mountain air and looked from side to side at the blue mountains flying past her. It was like she was a bird, and she'd never felt anything that made her feel that kind of freedom.

As she got closer to the other end, she looked up and noticed something she never expected to see. Standing on the platform at the other end of the zip line was Travis. At first, she was mad that Cooper had lied about him being in town. But then he reached down and lifted something up. She realized Kate was holding the other end of whatever it was.

As she got closer, she saw it was a sign. *"Mia, will you marry me?"*

Feeling like she couldn't breathe, she stared at it. And then she watched Travis put down the sign and get on one knee, holding a small black box in the air just as she landed on the platform. Some man she had never seen scooped her up and unhooked her quickly. When she turned, Travis was still there, looking up at her, holding the most beautiful diamond ring she'd ever seen. She caught Kate's eye, and she was already crying with a big smile on her face.

"What on earth?"

"Mia, I'm sorry. I made a huge mistake not telling you what was going on, but I want you to know I did it because I wanted to build something for our future. I wanted to build something for me and for you and for our future babies. I wanted to surprise you. I wanted to show you I was worthy of your love and your lifetime commitment to me. And you may decide that you'll never forgive me, never trust me again. But I would never forgive myself if I didn't get down on one knee right now and ask you to be my wife."

She stood there, her hand over her mouth, stunned into a kind of silence she'd never experienced before. The word yes was bouncing around inside of her head, but for some reason it wasn't coming out of her mouth. She felt like her heart was stuck in her throat.

"Mia? I think he wants an answer," Kate prodded.

"Yes!" she finally managed to say before a deluge of tears fell out of her eyes. He stood up, slipped the ring on her finger and then picked her up, twirling her around.

"So you forgive me?"

She looked down at her finger, shining with a beautiful diamond. "Yes, I forgive you. As long as you can forgive me for not speaking to you for so long."

He laughed. "From now on, we communicate no matter what. I will never keep something like that from you again."

She hugged him tightly, so thankful that her sister had forced her to go there and that Cooper had pushed her straight off of a platform and into the life of her dreams.

*A*s Mia stood in her bedroom, looking in the mirror, she couldn't believe that she was a bride. With her beautiful veil that belonged to her mother, and the gorgeous dress that she and Kate had picked out, she felt like the luckiest woman in the world. She couldn't wait to walk down the aisle and see Travis standing at the other end, probably with tears in his eyes.

She had opted to get married at the B&B, of course, because it meant more to her than anywhere else in the world. No church or venue could've held a candle to getting married in the place where she knew her mother's spirit was strongest.

She wished that her momma could've been there that day to help her get ready, to give her advice about marriage. But she knew that her spirit was in every part of the B&B. It had been only a month since Travis had proposed, but they had seen no reason to wait an extended period of time to get married. After all, they'd known each other longer than most people did when they got married.

"Those earrings are perfect," Kate said, coming up behind her in the mirror. Kate had found them in their mother's jewelry box as if they had been waiting there for Mia to wear on her wedding day.

"It's like Momma is here with me. I thought it would be sad for me today, but I really feel her. I think I feel her more today than I have felt her since she's been gone."

"I'm glad. I think I feel her too, even though I never met her."

"Knock, knock," their father said from the other side of the door. Jack and Sylvia had arrived last night, and Mia was so happy that her father was going to be there to walk her down the aisle. That was something that she had never thought would be possible.

"Come in," Kate said.

When Jack walked into the room, his eyes immediately filled with tears. "I can't believe how stunning you are. My little girl is getting married."

Mia hugged him, being careful not to rub her make-up on his black suit. "I'm so glad that you could be here, Dad. It's a miracle, and I think it came straight from Momma."

"She would be so proud of you, Mia."

"Are we ready?" Kate asked, looking at her watch.

Jack nodded. "We are. It's time to get you married off, young lady." Mia smiled up at him.

"Then let's get to it!"

They walked downstairs and then out into the backyard where everything had been set up. Mia didn't want a big wedding with a bunch of unimportant people. She only wanted those closest to her at her wedding. She invited some guests of the B&B that had been important to her over the years, a few friends from town and, of course, Lana had come.

Even though she had to come in between concerts, Lana said she wouldn't have been anywhere else. She had taken the redeye the night before and would fly out an hour after the wedding was over. Mia appreciated her friendship more than ever.

She had also agreed to sing at the wedding, using only an acoustic guitar. Mia couldn't wait to hear what she had prepared.

Kate and Evie had cooked all the food, and Cooper had set up the backyard in a way that looked like a fairytale with trellises, flowers and an arch that he'd built from reclaimed wood. Mia didn't know exactly what all he had done to make it look like some kind of Hollywood set, but she was thankful for his talent.

As the sliding glass doors opened, Kate first walked out to take her place at the front with a minister. Then the wedding march started to play, and Jack led his daughter to the edge of the patio.

"Are you ready?"

She smiled. "I've never been more ready for anything in my life."

She walked down the aisle, looking at Travis the whole time. The smile on his face was so big and bright. She couldn't believe her good fortune that she had found someone to love her like he did, but she would never take that for granted. Their love had spanned so many years, and she was thankful to have so many more in front of them.

"Who gives this woman to this man in holy matrimony?"

"Her mother and I," Jack said, smiling and winking at Mia. She almost burst into tears when she heard him acknowledge her mother like that.

He gave her hand to Travis before walking over to sit down in a chair in the front row next to Sylvia.

"You look stunning," Travis whispered.

"Thank you. You don't look so bad yourself," she said. She'd probably never see him in a tuxedo again, but she was enjoying it while she could.

Over the next few minutes, as the minister spoke about marriage, all Mia could think about was that she couldn't wait to start her life with him. She couldn't wait for their honeymoon to Scotland and Ireland. She couldn't wait to start having children. And she couldn't wait to see who she became as the years went on and she followed her dreams with her soulmate at her side.

They listened to Lana singing an original song, and Mia wiped away the tears. And then it was time to say I do, and the minister called for Travis to kiss his bride. When he dipped her to the side, she screamed a little, causing the guests to laugh. It was an incredible, memorable moment.

As the day and night wore on, there was eating, dancing and laughing. Her cheeks hurt from smiling so much. When it was all over, Mia didn't feel a sense of sadness that her wedding was over. Instead, she felt a sense of excitement that her life was just beginning.

I WOULD LOVE to connect with you! Feel free to join my private Facebook reader group at https://www. facebook.com/groups/RachelReaders and also visit my website for a complete list of my books at www. RachelHannaAuthor.com.

Made in the USA
Monee, IL
20 March 2022

93223107R10100